THE GOLDEN GHOULS

A PARANORMAL MYSTERY ADVENTURE

MONSTERS OF JELLYFISH BEACH 1

WARD PARKER

MAD MANGROVE MEDIA

CONTENTS

FOREWORD

I admit I love the feeling of family. My different series of novels stand alone, but they all have a familial connection. You can dive into and enjoy "Monsters of Jellyfish Beach" without having read any of my books. All references to Missy's back-story are fully explained. However, if you want to learn more about Missy's history, you can check out my earlier "Freaky Florida" series. Also, Missy pops up now and then visiting her cousin in the midlife paranormal "Memory Guild" series. More info at wardparker.com

Now, on to the main event...

PROLOGUE

I'm a witch, not a clairvoyant. I couldn't tell if the nightmare I just experienced was a premonition or simply a reaction from Taco Tuesday. But when I awoke from it, there was none of that blessed relief you feel when you realize it was a just a bad dream before falling asleep again.

No, I felt unsettled and full of dread. Like something wicked was coming.

My old-fashioned clock radio said 2:34 a.m. Brenda and Bubba, my two gray tabbies, studied me from the other side of my bed in the faint glow from the clock. I must have awakened them by moaning or something.

The dream had been about my mother. I had a relationship with her that could charitably be called difficult. I grew up with adoptive parents and didn't even know my birth mother was alive until a few years ago.

It turned out she was an evil sorceress.

I know what you're thinking: I'm a bitter daughter who calls her mother evil because I resent her.

No, it's because she's evil. Really. Our paths first crossed when I fought back against her black magic. And she tried to kill me.

Long story short, the Magic Guild in North Florida finally neutralized her, stripping her of her black-magic powers. Afterwards, we had an uneasy truce and remained distant. But at least she stopped trying to kill me. So, in that sense, you could say she was an absolutely wonderful mother.

That's why the dream I just had disturbed me. Because in the dream, she performed a ceremony with a demon. There was fire and blood, as well as sacrilegious acts I couldn't remember.

As if she had regained her black magic.

If true, what would she do with it?

Good thing I don't have to see her for the holidays.

CHAPTER I
A DAY AT THE BEACH RUINED

I had to face the truth: employers will be employers, and clients will be clients. They're all slaves to their instincts and selfish needs. And if I spend my life catering to their demands, instead of my own, I'm going to get burned.

Because in my job, I worked for and with monsters. Metaphorically and literally.

It was time to consider a career change. And here I was, spending my precious day off at the beach obsessing about it.

The beach was uncrowded, and atop my towel, I stood out like a tourist fresh off the plane from Siberia. Yes, despite living in Florida, I had the complexion of a corpse.

Why? Funny you ask. I work the aptly named graveyard shift. I'm a home-health nurse for elderly retirees, and the bulk of my patients are vampires who were seniors when they were turned. As you know, seniors both living and undead must retire to southern climes like Florida.

I've altered my life to fit into theirs. And I'm increasingly asking myself why.

It was late afternoon, the sun was no longer blasting me, and my skin was cooled by a gentle breeze from the southeast. A flock of sanderlings picked at tiny shells at the edge of the surf, racing away from the last gasp of each incoming wave. Not having been to the beach in so long, I studied the crowd.

There was a time when the only people you'd see on a day like this would be retirees, who lived in condos along the beach, and a few younger tourists. Only on the weekends would you see the folks who lived inland and worked at jobs managing the retirees' money, fixing their plumbing, or selling the goods they consumed.

Now, the crowd was more diverse in age. Jellyfish Beach had a new luxury hotel on the beach. More beachfront mansions were sprouting up, as were subdivisions on the mainland.

Everyone was moving to Florida, even monsters. Though our state already had plenty of home-grown monsters, not even counting our politicians.

My employer, Acceptance Home Care, was booming because they catered to the various species of supernatural creatures who hid their true identities. Despite their business doing so well, the company did not pay me well. I needed to work a part-time job at the Jellyfish Beach Mystical Mart and Botanica to help make ends meet. That's why having last night and this afternoon off was a rarity for me.

I became a home-health practitioner after years as an ICU charge nurse had burned me out. It seemed another burning out was just around the corner.

"Well, Missy, aren't you as pale as a vampire?" said a male voice above me.

It was Matt, my friend, partner in crime, and potentially more. Matt was a reporter for the local newspaper and knew about the secret existence of the vampires, werewolves, and other monsters I cared for. He had sworn to me he would keep the secret in exchange for my giving him a rare glimpse into the supernatural world. His investigative skills have come in quite handy when I've needed to solve mysteries of various sorts in this murky, dangerous world.

"You ready to go?" he asked.

We had planned to grab late-afternoon drinks and an early dinner at a nearby restaurant before I was due to give a vampire her annual physical.

"Don't you want to hang out on the beach for a bit?" I asked, though he was wearing jeans and a nice shirt.

"I was here at sunrise surf fishing. I've had enough sand for the day."

Matt used to arrive at the beach every morning before sunrise to fish until I told him the condo tower a mile away was filled with vampires. With that knowledge, he decided he'd wait until the sun crested the horizon.

I threw on a coverup, and we crossed the street. In Jellyfish Beach, the coastal road was right at the edge of the beach, providing easy access for the public. Across the street was a block of ocean-facing restaurants and a swim-apparel shop. The cafe on the corner was where we normally met for breakfast when I finished my shift, and he was about to begin his. Today, we were going to Clammy's, a boisterous beach bar we rarely had the chance to visit together.

He grabbed my hand as we crossed the street. It was sweet but silly. I let him do it anyway.

We found a table on the sidewalk facing the beach. Matt settled into a draft beer while I sipped a club soda. I would have preferred wine, but I had to work in a few hours.

"So," he said. "How's your magic going?"

While nursing is my profession, magic is my hobby. My passion, actually.

"It's barely going," I replied. "I've been too busy with work to practice my regular spells, let alone learn any new ones."

"Sorry to hear that." Matt had no interest in magic himself, but he appreciated it when my spells saved our butts from danger.

We were silent for a while, enjoying our beverages. The people walking on the sidewalk along the beach were enough to entertain us.

"Oh, give me a break," Matt said. "That guy has no business walking around in nothing but a Speedo."

An enormous man with an enormous gut strutted proudly by. His bathing suit was so small as to be almost invisible among all his flesh.

"He's an ogre, actually," I said.

"What? Are you serious?"

"Ogres can blend in among humans fairly well. You'd think he worked in construction or for the Mafia."

"I thought he was a former offensive lineman."

"The tip-off is where he missed with his spray-on tan. See the back of his legs?"

"His skin is greenish."

"Yep. And look at his ears."

"They're pointy. I didn't notice at first."

"He's probably wearing the skimpy bathing suit to distract people."

"Yeah, his face kind of looks like a caveman."

"That's an ogre for you."

"Are there a lot of them around here?"

"Not many," I said. "It's too hot here for them to live year-round. And they prefer Orlando for their vacations because they really love theme parks."

"Are there any other monsters walking by that my human eyes can't detect?"

"See that couple getting on the motorcycle?"

"Yeah?"

"The woman gives off the vibe that she's a werewolf. It's nothing in the way she looks—I just have a sixth sense for spotting supernatural creatures."

"It's a survival mechanism," Matt said.

"Absolutely. Well, we won't see any vampires at this hour. Trolls don't go out in public much. There could be other creatures who have shifted into human form that I'm not picking up on."

"You make people-watching much more interesting, now that I know not all of them are people. Hey, see that guy there with the purple shorts and no shirt? Is he a werewolf?"

"No. He's a guy who needs to have his back waxed before he takes his shirt off in public again."

"Agreed."

"Wait, I think that's a water sprite on the roof of the lifeguard stand."

"Where? There's just a seagull."

"Watch the gull closely."

He stared for a while with a puzzled expression until a grin broke out.

"Yes! I saw it, but only briefly."

"Sprites aren't shifters," I explained, "but they can cast magic to glamour human senses. It's sort of like camouflage."

"Are there any creatures here at the beach that could eat us?"

"Sharks."

"No," Matt insisted. "*Supernatural* creatures."

"The ogre could eat you, but he wouldn't do so in public. Same with the werewolf, of course. There are plenty of deadly creatures in Jellyfish Beach that would never come to the beach in daylight."

"That's not exactly reassuring."

"Listen, monsters must remain hidden to survive in the modern world. They're very discreet when it comes to eating people and do it rarely. Remember, a hundred and fifty years ago, when Florida was a wilderness, the pioneers were eaten by bears, alligators, panthers, and more. Face it, we, the apex predators, are sometimes prey. It's a fact most of us go through our lives without ever thinking about. It's better that way."

"Now, I can't *not* think about it."

My phone buzzed. I cursed when I saw the text from Acceptance Home Care.

"Speaking of monsters. Why are they bugging me? They know I have the afternoon off."

The text wanted to know if I was available for an emergency visit to Seaweed Manor. The condos were nearby, and I had several patients there. Reluctantly, I called the office.

"Sorry to bother you, Missy," said Brenda, the care coordinator. "It's Mr. Roarke, the HOA president. He asked for you specifically."

I sighed. Harry Roarke was a patient of mine, and if we angered him, he could cancel the contract with our agency.

"Okay." I sighed. "What kind of emergency is it?"

"He wouldn't say. Only that it was embarrassing and needed immediate attention."

From the frown on Matt's face, it was clear he knew what was going on.

"You're going to stand me up, right?"

"Yes. I'm sorry. I need to change my clothes first, and after I see the Roarkes, there won't be time to get back here to eat before my appointment with my vampire patient."

"I understand," he said sourly.

I'm afraid to say I've ditched Matt too many times before.

"I'll make it up to you."

"You need to make it up to yourself. You've been complaining about this job forever."

"I'm fond of most of my patients."

"I know you are. You're not fond of your employer, though. This job is killing you."

Little did he know how prophetic his words would prove to be.

CHAPTER 2

MY PATIENTS ARE MONSTERS

I ran home to change, then drove south on A1A, the coastal road that runs along the narrow strip of barrier island that separates the beaches from the mainland. In Jellyfish Beach, it was where you found condos and single-family homes facing the waterway to the west or the ocean to the east. Most were super expensive. The older condominium high-rises were slightly more affordable.

Among these were Squid Tower and Seaweed Manor. The former was the secret home of a community of vampires I served. Turned late in life, they moved down here for the warmth, but *not* the sunshine. The other community was for shifters, mostly werewolves, who were also retired and long in the tooth.

For all my patients, my biggest imperatives were to be discreet as well as compassionate. Monsters could be quite skilled at killing humans, but humans outnumbered them greatly and had plenty of weapons. Secrecy was the key rule of survival.

That's why I had my job. Monsters, even in human form, couldn't go to a doctor's office or a hospital without being found out. It would be difficult to hide the fact that you were undead from your primary-care physician. And even monsters with magical healing abilities needed healthcare from time to time.

In case you're wondering, the patient who had requested me, Harry Roarke, was a werewolf residing in Seaweed Manor. It was right next door to Squid Tower. The two communities did not get along.

There was no inherent enmity between vampires and werewolves. However, the vampires here were very tidy and rather snobbish. The werewolves were a bunch of party animals, pun intended, and they were not meticulous in caring for their community. I reflected upon this after almost tripping over an empty beer bottle near the bocce courts.

The Roarkes lived in A-714. Their hall was full of muffled rock music and the scent of weed. And I don't mean seaweed. I usually saw patients in this community late in the afternoon, before my nightly vampire visits, or in the mornings just after sunrise. No matter the time of day I showed up, people were always partying here.

"Thanks for coming by," Harry said at the door. "We have tickets for the new production at the Jellyfish Beach Playhouse, but we can't go with this, um, condition."

He led me into the living room. Cynthia waved hello from the couch but was too busy scratching herself to say anything.

Harry scratched at his heavy mane of silver hair and his

large white beard.

"Is it a rash?" I asked.

"Fleas," Harry replied. He instinctively tried to scratch himself with his leg dog-style but grew self-conscious with me staring at him.

"It's terribly embarrassing," Cynthia said. "We've had fleas before when in wolf form, but after you shift back to human and shower thoroughly, you can get rid of them. Not this time."

"We tried flea shampoo, but since it's made for dogs, it irritates our skin. What should we do?"

A flea jumped from his head to his shoulder, and I stepped back out of jumping range.

"Baking soda can help," I said.

"Tried that," Cynthia said. "Didn't work."

"I've heard diluted apple cider vinegar will get rid of fleas."

"For a few hours. Then they came back," said Harry. "We've tried every remedy we could find on the internet."

"You're a witch," Cynthia said. "Can't magic help us?"

Part of my passion for magic came from when I found ways to use it for healing patients. In my eyes, a benevolent purpose like this was the best possible use of magic.

"I bet it could," I replied. "I don't know any specific spells off the top of my head. There's a warding spell that will chase the fleas away, but they'll come back. I need to develop a spell or amulet that will take them off and keep them off."

The challenge excited me. My life felt stuck in a rut lately—especially when called in during my afternoon off for something as lame as fleas. However, experimenting with magic to solve the problem was inspiring. Using magic to help people—well, monsters—felt like a higher calling.

"In the meantime, can you try that warding spell?" Cynthia asked. "I don't want to miss the play tonight. We can't show up there scratching and having fleas jump onto other theatergoers."

"Gotcha. Let me draw a magic circle in your kitchen, and I'll be done in no time."

"Um, we just had new tile installed in there," Cynthia said.

"No problem. I'll use a dry-erase marker."

Yes, I carry them in a tote bag along with basic magic and medical supplies. I carry that tote bag with me wherever I go—even the beach.

I guess I really *am* stuck in a rut.

After I cast the warding spell, Cynthia and Harry each rushed to a different bathroom to shower while the fleas made their mass escapes.

"I'll work on a spell for a permanent cure," I called out after them.

I left their condo feeling a bit better about my career. Nothing against home-health nurses, but they basically manage your health. It's the doctors who decide on the plans for healing.

Magic, it seemed to me, was how I could climb to a higher level of healing than just managing symptoms. It was the key to giving my life more purpose.

You can't make a living at magic, though. I'm talking about *real* magic, not stage illusions. The only person I knew who made a full-time wage from magic was my mother when she performed black-magic sorcery for hire. In my dream last night, she was enthralled again to evil.

One thing I can promise: I will never be like my mother.

AFTER I FINISHED with the Roarkes, it wasn't long before sunset and my appointment with Mrs. Steinhauer in unit 608 of Squid Tower. With an immortal creature, annual physicals add up to a never-ending cash stream for my employer. All they did was set up the appointments and handle the billing.

I had to do the dangerous work.

"Hi, Missy, good to see ya," Mrs. Steinhauer said as she opened her door. She was a stocky widow who lost her husband in World War I, when they were both human. Never marrying again, she worked office jobs until retiring in her sixties. She moved to Florida where, after leaving Bingo Night at the Senior Center one night, she was attacked by a vampire and turned.

After that, she naturally moved to Squid Tower.

"I've got a little present for you." She giggled and handed me a small plastic cup with a green screw-on lid.

Vampires pee only a couple of times a week. Fortunately, Mrs. Steinhauer was thoughtful enough to have this cup waiting for me in the fridge.

"Thank you so much," I said. "Let's hope your creatine levels are normal this time." For some bizarre biological reason, low creatine levels were a serious health risk for vampires. They could be as dangerous as a sharpened wooden stake.

Next, once she was sitting comfortably in the living room, I wrapped the blood-pressure cuff around her beefy arm and inflated it. This is just like when a human gets her blood pressure tested, except for the numbers. Hers was thirty-five over twelve, healthy for her, though potentially fatal for a human.

Her heart rate was five beats per minute. Not bad at all for an undead person.

Now came the scary part—the blood draw. I mean, scary for me, not for her. The sight and smell of even their own blood can set off any vampire.

I came prepared, of course. A vampire-repelling amulet hung around my neck. So did a crucifix, even though that worked only for ex-Catholic vampires. With vampires of other denominations and faiths, it was useless. I also had a spell designed to make my blood unappetizing.

"Please squeeze the rubber ball," I said. "And look away. Whatever you do, don't look at the blood vial."

Vampire veins are notoriously difficult to find, but once I did, I inserted the needle and watched the dark—almost black —blood slowly ooze into the vial. Vampires required special needles, which were always in low supply.

"It's a beautiful night, isn't it?" I'm so bad at small talk. Especially when drawing blood from a blood-sucking fiend.

"It is. I have a shuffleboard match later tonight."

I didn't like the way her voice sounded. It was huskier than normal.

"Did the Blood Bus show up tonight?"

Oops, maybe I shouldn't have brought up the topic of feeding. I was simply hoping her appetite was sated for the evening. The Blood Bus was one of those blood-donation vehicles that show up at shopping centers and outdoor festivals. Except the blood that the donors expected would go to hospital patients was instead driven directly to Squid Tower in time for dinner, heated in a microwave, and served to residents who lined up as if it were a food truck.

"We all promised we'd feed after the shuffleboard match," Mrs. Steinhauer said, "so as not to give anyone a physical advantage."

Her voice sounded even huskier.

"Almost done." I willed her blood to ooze a little faster.

Laughter came through her front door from the outer hallway. Instinctively, Mrs. Steinhauer glanced in that direction, probably recognizing the voice.

As she turned away from the door, her eyes passed the vial filled with her black-tar blood.

She growled.

Oh, my. This was not good.

"Please look away, Mrs. Steinhauer."

Instead, she looked me straight in the eyes. She was trying to mesmerize me.

I yanked my eyes away. The blood vial needed to be put away safely before it was too late. I withdrew the needle, dropped it in a plastic disposal bin, and capped the vial.

A bead of blood appeared at the puncture site. Unlike with humans, you rarely need to tape a cotton swab to a vampire's arm.

Before I could do so, her arm was against her lips as she licked the drop of blood.

And she went from a prim and proper elderly lady to a voracious beast.

The blow from her backhand sent me flying across the living room, landing on the dining-room table.

Dinner was served.

CHAPTER 3
THE VAMPIRE CREATIVE WRITING GROUP

Mrs. Steinhauer leaped toward me as I squirmed off the dining table. I grabbed a chair to fend her off like a lion tamer. She growled and lunged at me again, trying to catch my eyes and make me submissive.

I thrust the chair into her while I frantically mouthed the words for a protection spell. I'm a traditional earth witch who prefers to use candles, pentagrams, and such when I cast spells. Doing it on the fly like this was not ideal. But I wanted to live.

Why wasn't the amulet working?

She dove at me, and this time, grabbed hold of the chair.

Yes, a vampire with a body age in her sixties was not as strong as a younger one. But she was still stronger than me. She easily tore the chair from my grasp.

I finished the incantation for the protection spell. But it didn't engage.

Time to hightail it out the front door. I feinted toward the bedrooms, then darted to the door. But as I clicked the deadbolt open, she seized my hair and pulled me toward her.

This had never happened with a patient before.

I punched her in the head, but it was too late. Cold, burning pain hit my neck as her fangs plunged into my flesh at my jugular vein. The vampire saliva quickly ended the pain. It enables vampires to drink leisurely.

Gray spots appeared in my vision, and I grew faint. I was done for.

The sugary notes of "Tie a Yellow Ribbon 'Round the Old Oak Tree" came from her cellphone lying on the coffee table.

The distraction interrupted her drinking.

"That must be Phyllis," she said.

I landed hard on the faux-wood veneer flooring as she hurried to her phone.

"Hello? Phyllis? Yes, I was. I'm just finishing up my medical appointment. Oh, really? Okay, I'll meet you there before the match. And don't forget to bring your needlepoint. *Ciao*."

Mrs. Steinhauer noticed me lying on the floor, and realization seeped into her eyes.

"Lordy, I don't know what came over me," she said. "I'm so sorry, Missy. It must have been my blood that did it."

"Right." I didn't have the strength to get up yet.

"I'm so sorry. This must happen to you all the time."

"No," I said. "It doesn't. If it did, I would have quit a long time ago. Maybe it's time for me to retire."

"No, don't say that. I would feel horrible if you quit because of me."

I sat up, as quickly as my dizziness would allow. "You fed on me."

"It was an honest mistake. A moment of weakness. I'm so sorry, dear."

Finally, I made it to my feet. "Mrs. Steinhauer, have a good evening and an enjoyable shuffleboard match. The service will call you if there's anything unusual about your results."

"Thank you for coming. See you again next year." She turned away and fiddled with her phone, already putting the incident behind her.

I slung my tote bag over my shoulder and left the condo. My hands trembled. I was tempted to call my manager and quit on the spot, but I told myself not to do anything rash. Fortunately, a mere bite wouldn't kill me, nor would it turn me into a vampire. Mrs. Steinhauer would need to drain me to death, then resurrect me with her own blood, to turn me.

This was a risky job, and I knew it when I first took it. At the time, though, it had seemed tame compared to what I had been through working in the ICU at the hospital. But tonight's incident had crossed the line.

There was a bottle of hand sanitizer in my bag, so I applied the gel liberally to my bite wounds as I rode down the elevator. Vampire mouth germs. Yuck!

I had no other patient appointments tonight, and I wanted to go home. But I had another commitment here at Squid Tower.

THANKS TO HAVING PUBLISHED a novel when I was younger, I had been pressured to lead a creative-writing critique group of vampires once a week. For my efforts, I was paid a paltry amount by the homeowners' association that was under pressure to keep the activity calendar full. Every last nickel came in handy with the salary I made—at my no-good, rotten, home-health nursing job.

I could text the group and tell them I was ill. The president of the association and adopted mother of the community, Agnes Geberich, would sympathize with my plight. But I didn't want to let down the members of the group.

When the elevator reached the lobby, I headed into the rear hallway that led to the community rooms. To my left, the larger room was filled with light and conversation. I walked in, and the ten vampires sitting in chairs arranged in a half circle looked up at me.

Their faces registered surprise.

"Missy, you poor girl! You've been bitten," said Gladys.

"Who did this to you?" Sol asked.

"You can tell that easily?" I asked. "I thought my collar covered the puncture wounds."

"Dear, we can tell just by smelling you," said Marjorie. "It's an ability we have that prevents us from feeding on someone else's prey. Vampires are very territorial."

"Thank you for your concern. A patient lost control while I was drawing blood."

"Tell me who it was," Sol demanded. "There needs to be accountability."

"I don't believe I can divulge that," I said. "You know, the HIPAA laws protect patient privacy."

"You were *assaulted* during a patient visit," Sol said. "HIPAA shouldn't apply."

"I don't want to get anyone in trouble."

"One of our bylaws says we're forbidden to feed on prey anywhere on the property. Especially on someone who is providing a valuable service. I'm going to report this to Agnes."

I was grateful to Sol for doing this. I simply nodded, though.

"Well, now that we have this all ironed out, would you guys like to hear part of my new short story?" Gladys asked.

"Missy almost gets drained, and you want us to listen to your soft-core porn?" Sol asked.

"It's not porn. It's erotic romance," Gladys said.

"I wasn't almost drained," I added. "I mean, I don't think I was."

"Iron," Doris said. "You need to consume lots of iron for your anemia."

"Anyway, it's a beach romance," Gladys said. "Beach romances are very popular nowadays. This one, though, takes place only at night."

"Let me guess," Sol said. "The heroine is a retired vampire living in a condo tower resembling this one."

"No. This is where I got truly creative. It's a *guest* visiting her vampire friend who lives in a condo tower resembling this one. And there's a vampire pool boy and a vampire delivery boy who both take a fancy to them."

"I honestly believe all your stories have a pool boy or a sweaty landscaper boy in them," Marjorie said.

"Of course," Gladys said. "Cold flesh, hot action!"

"Hence the label 'porn,'" Sol said.

"Let's let Gladys read her story," I interjected.

The vampire creative-writing group meetings were always

like this. No future Nobel Literature Prize laureates in the making here.

Many people take up writing when they retire. The folks here have endless years—centuries, even—to hone their craft and take their writing to another level. But they never do. No amount of coaching by me has made a difference.

"Sookie and Mary carried their towels and folding chairs to the beach," Gladys read from a paper manuscript, "when Sookie saw the DeadEx truck pull up to the building. The strapping driver, with pants too tight, jumped out of the truck. His package was gigantic. . . What's wrong, Missy? Was that word-play too on-the-nose? Your face just got paler."

I had sunken down in my chair. "Sorry. It wasn't your story, just the horrible experience I had tonight."

"I texted Agnes," Sol said. "She'll handle this flagrant rule-breaking properly."

"Yes, Gladys, the wordplay was like something a fourth grader would write," said Doris. "What has it been—a couple of centuries since you were in the fourth grade?"

Gladys cleared her throat theatrically and soldiered on. "'Isn't it time you took a lunch break?' Sookie asked the muscular driver. 'Come with us to the beach, and help us apply our sunscreen. Maybe it will stimulate your appetite.'"

Sol groaned. The other members looked uncomfortable.

I felt sick to my stomach. The thought of vampires eating was the last thing I needed in my head.

"I'll spare everyone the powerful but tasteful erotic scene," Gladys said. "Missy needs to rest. She had a traumatic experience tonight—thanks to one member of our community who was needlessly selfish."

"Thank you," I said. "We'll pick this up again next week."

I STAYED BEHIND to fold the chairs and stack them in the back of the room. Agnes appeared in the doorway. The woman with an aura of strength beyond her diminutive size was in her nineties in body age. That was how old she had been when she was turned in the year 497.

"Sol texted me what happened to you tonight," she said. "You poor dear."

"I'm all right. It was just a bit disconcerting."

"You were assaulted, and you lost blood. Who did this to you?"

"I can't say. Patient confidentiality."

"Nonsense. This has nothing to do with your patient's medical information. This was an assault while you were doing your job. I need to handle this because the association has a very expensive insurance rider to cover residents feeding on humans. If you don't tell me, Acceptance Home Care will, or else we'll cancel their contract."

"Okay. It was Mrs. Steinhauer. She didn't mean to do it. She saw the blood I was drawing from her and simply lost control."

"I'll take steps to improve your safety." She approached me, studying my face carefully. "Something else is wrong, am I right?"

I nodded. "Yeah, I think I'm burned out. I felt like this when I realized I had to quit working in the ICU. I love all you vampires and feel like I'm part of the community—as much as a human can be. But I'm tired of this job. I'm really over it."

"I understand, dear." Agnes patted my arm.

The elderly vampire, whom I towered over, was especially powerful. And I don't mean because she was the president of the HOA. She had major vampire powers, not to mention the wisdom of her over fifteen hundred years of existence.

There was no chance that Agnes would lose control of her appetite and bite me.

"I'm seriously considering quitting my job, Agnes. The pay is lousy. I'm tired of working the night shift. And I have the constant risk of what happened with Mrs. Steinhauer."

"What would you do instead?"

"I don't know. I could work for a hospital or an outpatient facility. It would be nice to have decent benefits again. Like a retirement account. Acceptance Home Care doesn't even offer that because they don't expect any employees to live long enough to retire. Don't laugh—I'm serious. The owner of the botanica where I work part time could give me more hours, but that job pays worse than this one."

Agnes seemed deep in thought. "Come with me to the terrace," she said.

I followed her down the hall to the door that led outside to a patio near the swimming pool. We each took a seat at a nearby table and stared at the reflection of the moon on the ocean. It was a full moon. I was sure of that because occasional howls came from the werewolves in Seaweed Manor next door.

How did I get myself into this life filled with monsters? Even my ex-husband, God rest his soul, ended up turning into a vampire. That was after he left me for his vampire boyfriend, and before I joined Acceptance Home Care. It was even before I got seriously into witchcraft. I just seemed to be drawn to monsters.

"I've decided to connect you with some individuals I know," Agnes said. "They run a philanthropic society and offer grants to those who help them."

I couldn't imagine how Agnes would be involved with them. After all, the root of the word "philanthropic" comes from the Ancient Greek for "man loving." Not "undead-creature loving."

"What's the focus of their philanthropy?" I asked.

"Cryptozoology."

"Say what?"

"In the most simplistic terms, it's the search for, and study of, cryptids—creatures that are believed to exist but aren't recognized by science. Also known as monsters. Creatures like me, the werewolves next door, and Bigfoot."

Oh boy, here we go again. Monsters.

"Their mission fits right in with what you've already been doing in helping us vampires and the other creatures you care for," Agnes explained. "As the world gets more crowded, there's increased danger of clashes between humans and supernatural creatures. And it will only end badly for us. This organization keeps track of the creatures who are out there, protects them, and makes sure their existence remains a secret and they stay hidden."

"I see. Now, did you mention grants?"

"Yes. Perhaps they can set you up so you don't have to work in a hospital again."

I can't deny that I was very intrigued. As much as I've complained about my life with monsters, they've changed me.

I'm not a normal person who could thrive as a regular nurse anymore. I've had a lot of contact with many bizarre creatures that shouldn't exist.

Plus, I have my magic. It's hard to imagine spending my lunch break in the hospital cafeteria chatting about TV shows, while I actually spend my free time dealing with the ghost who inhabits my house, creating magic spells, and bonding with vampires on their oceanfront terrace.

"Thank you," I said. "Please connect me with these people. Or whatever creatures they are."

CHAPTER 4
BOTANICA BLUES

It would have been nice to have a day off after being bitten by a vampire. But no, I was scheduled to open the botanica in the morning. And we opened painfully early. Why would a shop selling spiritual and magical paraphernalia need to open at 7:00 a.m.? To serve people before they went to work.

Hate your boss? You can pick up a voodoo doll to curse him or her during your commute to the office. Have a big client meeting today? We have just the potion to help your business succeed. Do you work in a dangerous job? We sell various charms to protect you.

As I opened the steel hurricane shutters we used for security at night, I found a zombie wedged into the corner. But it was just Carl.

"Morning, Carl," I said, unlocking the front door.

He moaned mournfully in his best attempt at a cheerful

greeting. He had been a Haitian professor in his sixties when he died and was brought back by Madame Tibodet. Still clad in his black funeral suit, he was a nice guy if you could overlook the decaying flesh.

Madame Tibodet, a voodoo priestess we work with, must have sent him here to pick up something for her.

"Go get what you need but show it to me before you leave."

He moaned and shuffled into the dark store. I turned on the overhead lights, even though he didn't need them. Reanimated corpses rely more on scent and feeling than vision.

The crash of a ceramic figurine shattering on the floor made me sigh. Just because zombies can get around in the dark didn't mean they weren't clumsy.

I swept up the pieces of Chango, the Santeria spirit of lightning, thunder, and fire. I added the figurine to Madame Tibodet's tab.

Carl had distracted me from the most important task when opening the botanica each day: winding up the ancient grandfather clock.

The clock had come with the botanica when Luisa bought it years ago from an obeah sorcerer. He told her the antique was from the Caribbean island of Martinique. Originally fabricated in Europe centuries ago, it was brought to the island by a sugarcane planter and refurbished with local mahogany.

It was also enchanted with magic I could feel but not identify. Luisa didn't know what it was, nor did Madame Tibodet or the other priests and witches who shopped here. No one knew who brought the clock to the US, but it was said to have been in this store for nearly a hundred years, since this building was originally built as a pineapple storehouse.

The clock has a powerful, scary legend around it. Namely, it must never be allowed to wind down and stop. Never. Ever.

Or else.

The botanica's previous owner claimed that if the clock stopped, the world would end. Luisa believes that if it stops, she will die. Our customers have dozens of different theories.

All I knew was we had to wind the darned thing every day. Or else. I opened the glass panel beneath the face, behind which the pendulum swung back and forth, and pulled on the chain that wound the gears. I was pretty sure the clock would last a few days without winding, but no one wanted to take that chance. After the laborious process, I opened the glass of the face and moved the minute hand four minutes forward, because the clock always ran slow.

As I listened to the heavy, doom-filled ticks of the ancient clock, I had a thought. What if we allowed the clock to run slow, getting behind by four more minutes every day? Would that somehow add more time to our lives?

Best not to mess with fate, I decided.

Carl shuffled to the counter. He held a vial of Florida water wrapped in his fingers with their horrendously long nails.

I added the item, the American version of *Eau de Cologne,* used like holy water by many of our customers, to Madame Tibodet's always-lengthy tab.

"Thank you, Carl. Be careful crossing the street."

He moaned and shuffled outside. You'd think a zombie going down the sidewalk would create a panic, but the truth was, he didn't look or walk much differently than many of the senior citizens trudging to the nearby bagel shop.

"Missy, you look tired," Luisa, the botanica's owner, said as she walked in later that day. She was a beautiful Afro-Cuban who served as her shop's resident Santeria priestess.

"Thanks a lot."

She laughed. "Don't worry, you still look younger than your years."

"I've been under a lot of stress lately," I said. "Made worse by having a patient feed on me."

"*Dios mio!*"

I explained what had happened.

"You should sue her."

"I don't believe I can. There's something about that in my employment contract."

We had little time to chat, because the shop's traffic would pick up soon at the beginning of the evening rush hour. Evenings saw busy sales in love potions, incense, and candles, as well as figurines of Santeria orishas and voodoo gods. Hobbyist witches usually came in around now to pick up ingredients for spells and amulets. Charms to dispel evil spirits flew off the shelves at this time of day.

Luisa and I both served customers and managed the register. When Luisa performed a brief Santeria ceremony in the back room, I covered for her. Normally, I worked this late shift before heading to the beach to see my patients. Tonight, blessedly, I had off.

Right before I left, Luisa took me aside.

"I didn't have time to talk to you earlier, but I need to next time you come in."

"Is something wrong?" I asked.

"I might have to close the botanica."

"That's horrible! Why?"

"The sleazy landlord is raising the rent, and revenues are down. The wholesale prices of all the inventory keep going up."

"Why is he raising the rent? He hasn't improved the building."

"He's raising it simply because he can."

The Jellyfish Beach Mystical Mart and Botanica was in a not-so-nice retail plaza in a not-so-nice neighborhood. Botanicas are common in South Florida and other places with large Latin and Caribbean populations, but you never find them in high-end malls. No, this botanica was sandwiched between a convenience store and a scary-looking seafood-takeout joint. Hardly a luxurious setting, but it was fairly safe and patronized by honest, working-class people.

"I'm so sorry to hear that," I said. "Is there any way I can help?"

She paused for a moment. "Invest and become a partner."

I laughed.

"No, I'm serious," she said.

"My savings are awfully meager. Pretty pitiful, to be frank, for being in my mid-forties. Most of the money is tied up in—"

"I'm sorry. I didn't mean to put you on the spot."

"It's okay. I've always been a wage slave. Never thought much about being an entrepreneur."

"Some witches get paid for their services, you know. You could do that through the store. We could sell more witchcraft supplies, too, for Wiccans, kitchen witches, hedge witches, and others. You could help me expand the clientele."

"What kind of investment would you need?"

Luisa grimaced. She had light-brown skin and tightly braided hair. Her nose was delicate and flared at the nostrils.

"It would have to be in the six figures."

That deflated me. "Sorry, but I simply can't come up with that much cash unless I win the lottery or something. Do you have any potions or charms for that?"

She handed me a small brown bottle with a handwritten label that said "good luck" in French.

"Let me know if you win," she said with an ironic smile.

"Believe me, I will."

I seemed to lose at everything else.

AFTER FEEDING the cats and myself, I settled down with a cup of tea to search my grimoires for a spell to cure the Roarkes of their flea problem.

The doorbell rang. I went to the door and peeked from the left sidelight. A man and woman of matching heights stood beneath my porch light. I opened the door a crack. "Can I help you?"

"Ms. Missy Mindle?" the man asked. He had the jet-black hair, light-brown skin, and round eyes of Central American indigenous descent. He held a black attaché case.

"Yes?"

"I am Mr. Lopez. This is Mrs. Lupis. We are from the Friends of Cryptids Society of the Americas and were referred to you by Agnes Geberich."

The woman also had black hair but was Caucasian. Both of them wore gray business suits with gray neckties. Both smiled, but in a constrained, formal way.

"I'm sorry, I didn't expect you so soon," I said. "Agnes mentioned you only last night."

"May we come in?" Mrs. Lupis asked.

"Oh, yes, please forgive my manners." I opened the door. "Would you like some coffee or tea? I can throw some together quickly."

"We'll have whatever you are having," Mrs. Lupis said. Her accent was vaguely European, but I couldn't place it.

"Then, tea it is."

When they came inside, I gestured toward the living room and asked them to have a seat. But they followed me to the kitchen and sat at the table while I put water on to boil.

"We will be direct," Mr. Lopez said. "Mrs. Geberich told us you are a practicing witch with moderate paranormal abilities, such as telekinesis. She said you have had extensive exposure to supernatural and mythological creatures. Is that correct?"

"Yes."

"You have not shared this exposure with other humans?"

"Correct. Only with the owner of the botanica where I work part-time. And my friend and collaborator Matt Rosen. He's a reporter who has encountered many of these creatures himself and has promised me to keep them secret."

"A reporter?" Mrs. Lupis frowned.

"Yes, but hard news. No tabloid stuff. He couldn't publish any information about the creatures, even if he wanted to, without losing credibility and ruining his career."

"If he does so, it will void the contract," Mrs. Lupis said.

"Contract?"

"Yes," Mr. Lopez said, placing his attaché case on the table and withdrawing documents. "The contract establishing a partnership between you, your retail establishment, and the Friends of Cryptids Society of the Americas."

"My retail establishment?"

"You called it a botanica," Mrs. Lupis said.

"How do you know about it?"

"We've already done the necessary vetting of you and your future partner, Mrs. Luisa Dominguez."

I was dumbfounded.

"Our foundation is providing you and your partner each with a grant of three million dollars." He pulled an envelope from the case with a check showing through the plastic window. "This should keep the retail establishment in business and allow you to become an owner. It will also enable the business to expand to better serve our purposes."

My mind was reeling. "Agnes said you deal with monsters?"

"We conduct regular censuses of the populations of monsters and creatures of myth and folklore. All the entities talked about in legends, but which do not officially exist. We lobby extensively to keep them from the attention of humans."

"We also protect them from extinction," Mrs. Lupis said. "Which is not to say we protect them from accountability. While we work to ensure no species is wiped from the face of the earth, we do not protect bad actors. If any creature kills humans or livestock excessively, threatening to reveal the actual existence of its species, we do not prevent the creature from being disciplined or destroyed."

"It's not as if we're PETA for monsters," Mr. Lopez said, smiling at his own joke. I didn't laugh.

"Why are you interested in the botanica?" I asked.

"It's a natural nexus of the supernatural community," Mrs. Lupis said. "Believers in the supernatural and paranormal congregate there. Followers of less mainstream religions go there. And where believers go, so go their supernatural beings."

"To be quite frank," her partner added, "the mainstream faiths in America all have supernatural creatures in their folklore, but the institutions have become so commercial and sanitized that the folklore has been pretty much stamped out. Except among the most fervent—or delusional—believers. A store selling Bibles, for instance, would not attract demons."

"So, you think the botanica will attract creatures?"

"Yes," Mrs. Lupis said. "As will your customers. And as you'll see in the contract, you will be obligated to encourage this."

So sick I was of my home-health career, I was extremely open to this offer. Should I hire a lawyer to study the contract?

"The contract is secret and cannot be shared with other individuals, including attorneys," Mr. Lopez said.

How did he read my mind?

"This grant is very generous," I said. "Is your society actually buying the botanica?"

"Absolutely not," he said. "Our grants support those who share and enact our mission. You, Miss Mindle, are the epitome of such an individual."

"The money goes to me or to the botanica?"

"It goes to you to invest in the botanica. You will keep

whatever is left over to begin a nest egg for yourself that you are so sorely lacking."

My face grew warm from embarrassment.

"How do you know about my finances?"

"We do our due diligence," he said. "The cash will pay for your partnership with Mrs. Dominguez. She is receiving the same deal as you. We have already audited the business and believe these funds should be sufficient to make the business flourish."

"Is she aware of this?"

"She has already signed the contract. Also, to sweeten the deal, we will pay the business annual bonuses if you catalog a required minimum number of creatures. Plus, we are purchasing the retail plaza for you, so the business won't have to deal with a landlord anymore."

"How can you have done all this work already?"

"We visited Mrs. Dominguez just before you. And we are in negotiations with the landlord. Let's just say he will not refuse."

"Wow."

"All that remains is for you to sign the contract and deposit your check."

I took the pen he offered.

"How can I be sure this isn't a deal with the devil?"

Both laughed.

"There are so many devils," Mrs. Lupis said with a smile. "Why would you make a deal with only one?"

I wasn't sure what she meant, but it didn't stop my signature crawling across the dotted line like a snake I couldn't control.

Just over two weeks later, I was the co-owner of the Jellyfish Beach Mystical Mart and Botanica. And I was a former employee of Acceptance Home Care. I promised all my patients that while I would no longer handle their regular health visits, they could always call me for advice or services on a cash basis.

They were noticeably disappointed but vowed to hire me for special needs, such as the flea solution for werewolves. I guess I was a better nurse than I had realized.

Despite all my additional responsibilities as a business owner, I agreed to continue running the vampire creative-writing workshops. No resident in Squid Tower was willing to do it, it seemed. I was happy to do so because it wasn't a big investment in time, and it allowed me to stay connected to the crotchety old vampires that I had become quite fond of over the years.

I did make a stronger vampire-repelling amulet, though. Hopefully, there wouldn't be any blood spilled at the workshops to make the vampires lose control, but overly purple prose might do it. You can never be too safe.

Luisa and I began planning how we would expand the botanica's offerings.

"According to the contract, we need to attract supernatural creatures?" Luisa asked.

"Not directly. We need to offer more products and services to attract more people who believe in them. Supposedly, then, the creatures will come."

"Come and do what?"

"Hopefully, not kill us."

"Are you sure this is a good idea?" Luisa asked.

"It's better than drawing vampire blood, I can tell you that. Look, all we need to do is make a record of the creatures we encounter. And help them if they need it."

"Help them how?"

"We'll see."

CHAPTER 5
DEAD ON ARRIVAL

"Where is my stuff?" I said aloud in my living room one evening as I clicked the tracking button of my internet order over and over.

Out for delivery, it told me over and over. But it was getting late.

In the United States of America, one of the few things we can agree on is we want the junk we buy on the internet to be delivered fast and on time. The delivery services are ruthlessly efficient at this.

However, packages occasionally are lost. Or something much, much worse happens.

My cats, Bubba and Brenda, looked at me with expressions that implored me to chill out. They didn't realize how impatient I felt. I had cobbled together various ancient potion recipes into one that I hoped would make werewolves permanently free of fleas. It was an old-school-style potion made from weird and disgusting ingredients. The kind that fit the stereotype of an old crone stirring eye of newt into a cauldron.

In my case, I needed fur of muskrat. And it had to be freshly shaved from a living muskrat's belly. I know, pretty specific— but that's the way magic works.

I don't know how to catch a muskrat. And even if I did, I don't have the fortitude to shave its belly.

That's why I needed my overnight delivery from a witches-supply company in northern Wisconsin. And I needed it tonight, as was promised. The Roarkes had been waiting for my cure and were losing patience.

So where was my stuff?

My head jerked toward the front windows when I heard the distinct rumbling and gear-grinding of the sort of large van used by UPP, the delivery company. It came from just up the street, then stopped. One of my neighbors must be getting a delivery, as well.

I eagerly waited. My potion was simmering in a stockpot— my version of the cauldron—on a propane burner in the garage. That's where I make the fouler-smelling brews, and this one ranked near the top in noxiousness. All it needed was the fresh muskrat fur to be whisked in, and the potion would be complete and ready for the spell to activate it.

You're probably wondering why someone who just received a check for three million would still want to treat werewolves for fleas. Because of the thrill of healing with magic, that's why.

So, where was that delivery? I opened the front door to make sure it hadn't appeared on my porch without my hearing it. Nope. I glanced up the street and saw the UPP truck still idling at a house two doors away.

I walked closer to the street to be at an angle where I could see the neighbor's front porch. The light was on, but no one stood outside the door. Did my neighbors invite the driver into their house?

A family of single elderly women lived there, three sisters with the last name of Osman. Some neighbors jokingly called them "The Golden Girls," after the old TV sitcom. I weighed the possibility that the driver was inside performing a striptease for the eager ladies. If it was a he, that is.

It might have been believable except for the tight schedule these delivery companies give their drivers. No time for bathroom breaks means no time for hanky-panky.

I figured the driver was sitting in the truck's cab, scrolling on his handheld scanner. Or in the back, rearranging packages. Why not just walk to the truck and get the dang package?

I walked over, and there was no driver in the cab.

"Hello?" I called. "Are you in the back?"

No answer. There was no light on in the rear, so the driver couldn't see to do anything back there. Was he napping?

Though I was sure I was breaking several rules, I got onto the first step leading to the cab and leaned in. A little ambient light from the streetlamp made it into the back through the translucent roof. I didn't see anyone but couldn't be completely sure. And going back there to look for my package was surely out of bounds.

I stepped back onto the street and glanced at my neighbor's house again.

Wait, was that a package lying on the front lawn?

I walked up to the medium-sized box lying on its side. My neighbor's address was on it.

It appeared the driver had dropped the box there during his walk to the front door and then simply disappeared. Maybe he needed a bathroom break really badly.

I glanced over at the hedge on the property line and froze as I realized what I saw.

A foot wearing an athletic shoe and a brown sock with the UPP logo. Above the foot was a hairy leg sticking out of men's shorts. I moved closer, compelled to check if I could give him medical assistance. I was a nurse, after all.

Once I reached the foot, I realized that no, I could not offer assistance.

Because all that lay before me was the foot and the leg. The rest of the driver was nowhere to be seen.

"Oh, my," I said aloud.

Yes, time to call 911.

AFTER THE POLICE and first responders arrived, I did what neighbors always do in a similar situation: stand around the crime scene, attempt to get information, and make up all varieties of wild, uninformed theories.

"Are you sure it's not a prosthetic limb?" asked Old Man Timmons from across the street.

"I'm sure," I said.

"Fred Furman, who lives behind this house, thinks the old ladies are cannibals," said a slouching middle-aged guy I didn't recognize.

"Don't be a moron!" the woman next to him said.

"I bet a gator came out of the canal and got him," Jocelyn, one of my immediate neighbors, said.

It seemed to me like the most logical explanation so far.

"I rarely see any gators in there," said Old Man Timmons, who lived on the canal. "And I've never seen one cross the street."

"It's mating season, you know," said Jocelyn.

"You're implying the gator was trying to mate with the delivery driver? That's kind of sick if you ask me," said someone in the crowd.

"It was probably a drive-by shooting. Those happen everywhere these days," the slouchy moron said.

"And his leg came off?"

"Yeah. The bullets from those assault rifles can do that."

"I didn't hear any gunshots."

"Neither did I."

The speculation went on, seemingly forever, until a female cop in a Jellyfish Beach Police uniform came out of the house and approached me.

"You're the one who found the body?"

"Yes," I said. "I mean, I found the leg. I don't know where the rest of him is."

"No one does. Please come inside and speak to the detective."

I followed her through the front door just as an SUV labeled Crime Scene Investigation pulled up, followed by a rundown pickup truck belonging to Matt. He probably heard about the incident on his police scanner and recognized the street name. That would explain the multiple texts from him I hadn't had time to read.

When I entered the house, I saw the three sisters sitting at the dining-room table. I would guess they ranged in age from early sixties to early eighties. They wore strained expressions that probably came from being questioned. The detective, another woman, in a Jellyfish Beach Police Department polo shirt approached me.

"Please have a seat in here," she said, gesturing to a chair in the living room that was covered with protective plastic— clearly intended to preserve the putrid mustard color of the fabric—that made my skin stick to it as soon as I sat down.

The detective was young enough to make me suspicious of her skill level. In my mid-forties, I had enough miles on me to have earned the right to be skeptical of the very young.

She asked for my name and introduced herself as Detective Shortle.

Shortle was not short; in fact, she had the physique of a basketball player and the attitude of one who played rough. Her black hair was in a ponytail, pulled so tight it appeared to stretch her expression into fierceness. She had pretty, olive skin and a narrow face with prominent cheekbones.

"You found the remains?" she asked me.

"Yes."

"Why? Why were you in this yard near the hedge?"

"I was wondering why my package was late. The van was parked in front of this house forever, so I walked over and saw a package lying on the lawn. When I went to retrieve it for the Osmans, I saw the leg."

She seemed to grasp for something else to ask.

"I don't know the delivery driver," I said, to be helpful. "All I know is what shoes he wears."

"Do you know the Osmans well?"

"No. Only waving to them from the driveway, that kind of thing."

"Okay." She pretended to write notes on a small pad. "Have you seen any suspicious characters in the neighborhood?"

"No. It's very quiet here. It helps that we're a cul-de-sac."

"I see." She looked up with relief when the front door opened.

"Good gracious, it's a boneyard out there!" announced a pudgy man with helmet-like hair and a Jellyfish Beach Police polo shirt.

"Excuse me?" the detective asked.

"We found skeletal remains. Obviously, not belonging to the current victim."

The three sisters gasped. So did I.

"Where?" the detective asked.

"In the backyard. In a leaf bag sitting on a bed of petunias. The remains of several individuals."

"Of other delivery drivers?" I asked. "I've been having problems with late packages."

"I don't know who they were, only that they appear to have been devoured."

The sisters gasped again.

"We'll need to run tests to confirm that," he added.

"What could have done this?" I asked. "We don't have any large carnivorous animals around here."

In truth, I once had a baby dragon that I rescued from the Everglades living in my garage. He didn't eat humans, though. Only iguanas. And mangos.

"We'll have to run tests," the tech said.

I studied the three sisters in the dining room. There was something off about them. Maybe cannibalism wasn't such a stupid theory after all.

The detective asked for my phone number, gave me her business card, and slipped out of the house. From the front window, I saw Matt pestering her with questions while she tried to make her way to her car.

"Can I offer you something, dear?" asked the eldest sister. She was small and wiry, with hair dyed an unnatural blonde.

"No thanks, I'm good." I hoped she wouldn't offer me a meat pie. "I'm Missy. We've met before, but it was years ago, in the aftermath of the last hurricane."

Nothing brings neighbors together more than a natural disaster. Or human remains in a yard.

"Yes," said the middle sister, in her seventies. "We don't see you much. You keep odd hours."

"I used to work nights a lot as a home-health nurse." I left out that my hours had been mandated by vampire patients.

The sisters introduced themselves. The youngest one, June, was in her sixties. May was the middle one. The eldest should have been named April, in my opinion, but her name was Alex.

"Do you guys have any idea who or what killed the driver?" I asked.

All three shook their heads.

"Do you have a doorbell camera or any sort of security monitoring?"

They shook their heads again.

"The package was just a pair of shoes," said June. "The poor man was killed for delivering shoes that I'll probably return."

Her eyes welled with tears, and Alex patted her arm. I found it interesting that June and May let their hair go white while their older sister had dyed hers.

Outside, Detective Shortle had finally extricated herself from Matt and sat in her car talking on a handheld radio. Matt let himself into the house without knocking.

"Hey, wow, how are you, ladies? I'm Matt Rosen with *The Jellyfish Beach Journal*. Do you have a moment?"

"Are we allowed to talk to the press?" May asked.

"I don't know," Alex said. "No press has ever wanted to talk to us before. Are you here to ask about the murder?"

"He's here to sell a newspaper subscription," I muttered. Matt grinned at me.

"Yes, the murder," he said. "And I hear there are remains of other victims in your garden."

"I weeded that garden two weeks ago, and there weren't body parts in it," June said.

"The crime scene tech told me the bones were in a leaf bag," Matt said. "They will have to be tested to determine their age. Do you have a landscaper who may have accidentally dug them up?"

"They only maintain the lawn, not our gardens," Alex said.

"I'm sure the police asked you if you've seen any suspicious characters around the neighborhood."

"They did, and we haven't."

"This is disturbing for a pleasant neighborhood like this," Matt said.

"You've got that right, speaking as someone who lives two houses down," I said. Being a witch, and having the home-health patients I've had, I see disturbing things. But nothing that would get me on a true-crime TV show like these murders could.

A car parked behind Detective Shortle's. A stocky, bald man got out and was joined by Detective Shortle. They both approached the house.

The doorbell rang. June hurried over and opened it.

"Oh, you're back?"

"Ms. Osman, this is my colleague, Detective Glasbag," Shortle said. "We would like you and your sisters to ride with us to the police station to talk in greater depth."

"Oh. Are we under arrest?"

"Not at all," Detective Glasbag said. "We just want to talk."

"It's awfully late," May protested.

"I'm in the middle of binge-watching a reality show," Alex added.

"We'll make it brief," Shortle said. "And drive you home immediately."

Matt and I took our cue and left while the ladies were fussing with gathering their handbags and sweaters. "In case it's cold at the police station," Alex said.

"Do you think they're suspects?" I asked Matt.

"Of course. They wouldn't be the first sweet elderly ladies to be murderers."

I didn't mention this, but I realized what it was about the sisters that had struck me as odd.

The cold, almost predatory, look in their eyes.

CHAPTER 6

CAN GHOULS BE VEGANS?

The night of the murder, I never got my package. I had a stockpot full of a noxious potion that I had to remove from the propane burner and refrigerate. It went into the second fridge I keep in the garage, with the cans of soda and beer for guests, along with magic-making ingredients, such as the bottle of water from the River Nile, a box of graveyard dirt, and the packages of nasty bits from rodents that a witch friend gifted me.

Early the next morning—too early, if you ask me—a *thump* sounded on my front porch and the doorbell rang. I opened the door wearing a robe and found the delayed package lying there. The delivery truck was still idling in front of my house as the driver climbed into the cab while studying his hand-held scanner.

"Excuse me," I said, walking briskly across my lawn.

The driver looked up at me and knocked me off guard with his good looks. He was an older guy, with short-cropped graying hair, lean and fit but not in his prime like many of the drivers.

My theory was that their delivery careers lasted only until their backs began needing surgery. Which was thanks to customers like me who order pet food that comes in 100-pound boxes.

"Morning," I said. "Thanks for getting my package to me today. I'd been expecting it yesterday, but... Can you tell me anything about the driver who was killed on this street last night?"

"My apologies for the delay, ma'am. This is my normal route, but they sent an extra truck out yesterday to handle the overload. I wasn't told I was delivering any of those packages today. And no one told me about anyone being killed." His beautiful blue eyes searched mine quizzically.

"This is your normal route? Sorry about ordering all the cans of cat food."

He smiled. "I've survived this job for so long because I use a hand truck. I'm not like those foolish young bloods who carry the Gooey-dot-com boxes on their shoulders."

"So, there's no gossip at the warehouse about the driver?"

"I'm sure there is, ma'am. I'll have to ask around. They treat us like we're disposable, so I'm not surprised I haven't heard anything from management. If I do, I'll let you know, if you're home when you get your next package."

"Thank you. Be safe."

I brought my box inside. The large box contained air packets and the tiny box of the actual product, the muskrat belly fur. My potion would have to wait, because I had a busy day and evening ahead of me.

WHEN I ARRIVED at the botanica, Luisa's brow was furrowed as she studied her copy of the contract with the Friends of Cryptids Society.

"You don't look like a carefree millionaire," I said.

"What about Clause 15 in Part 2, Section B?"

She pointed to the clause, almost punching a hole in the paper with her finger. I pulled my copy from a tote bag and looked up the clause.

"Oh. We're supposed to 'find justice for those creatures who deserve it and mete out justice upon those who have committed transgressions.'"

"Yes. I take transgressions to mean killing people."

"Don't look at it so negatively," I said. "It could also mean minor crimes."

"Like monsters illegally parking?"

"Better it be us than a cop, right?"

"And what does it mean by finding justice for those who deserve it?" she asked.

"I'm not sure. Help monsters who are victims of crime? Exonerate monsters who are unjustly accused of crimes?"

"We don't have the skills or resources to be a supernatural police force."

"Of course not. But I've investigated some mysteries in the past, with the help of my friend Matt."

"Are you saying you'll be a private detective for monsters?"

"If I have to, and if they have no one else to turn to. But let's hope it never comes to that."

Well, it did come to that. Only one day later.

The bells tinkled at the front door as someone entered the incense-filled shop. By the way, we need to cut down on the incense. It creates havoc with my sinuses now that I'm here all day long.

Anyway, the customer who entered the shop was none other than the youngest of the three Golden Girls, June. She stopped, puzzled, in front of a *Demon-Be-Gone* spray bottle. According to the label, it removes stubborn stains and powerful demons.

"Hi, June," I said with my warmest smile. "What brings you here? You and your sisters didn't strike me as the types who shop at a place like this."

"I'm sorry, but I'm not here to shop for demon remover." She laughed nervously. "It's about another matter."

"Is it about the, um, incident at your home?"

"Yes."

"I don't know how I can help you. And how did you even know I work here?"

"Word gets around quickly in our community."

"You mean our neighborhood?"

"No," she said. "Our community. The supernatural community."

Luisa chose this moment to come out of the back room. She must have been eavesdropping. I introduced her to June.

"You're involved with the supernatural?" I asked June incredulously. "Are you and your sisters witches?"

"No, though I admit it would fit a stereotype if we were."

"Are you . . . not human?"

She nodded with a sheepish smile. "We're ghouls. We shape-shift to our human forms most of the time."

"Why did you choose to appear as seniors?"

"Because these are the forms of the last people we ate."

She couldn't miss seeing my eyes widen.

"It was years ago."

You won't believe this, but I had encountered ghouls before. A bunch of them moved down here from New Jersey and created a big problem by raiding the cemeteries for corpses. If you're not familiar with ghouls—and I hope you are not—they're basically demonic monsters, originally from the deserts of the Middle East, who, well, eat people.

Luisa, though, had never met a ghoul before. Her face turned ashen, and she backed away slightly from June.

"Don't worry," June said. "We try so very hard not to attack living people anymore."

The word "try" didn't make me feel any better. Especially since I knew ghouls would indeed eat people, living or dead.

Okay, so things had gotten rather awkward. What are you supposed to say when someone tells you they abstain from eating people?

"Good for you," I said.

"We believe the police suspect us of the murder of the delivery driver," June said. "And of the other victims whose remains they found in our backyard."

"Do they know that you're ghouls?"

"No, and we can't allow them to find out. And they will find out if we end up in jail. We can maintain our human forms for only so long."

"Have the police charged you with anything yet?" Luisa asked.

"Not yet. Our lawyer thinks they will soon, even though he doubts they have any evidence."

"Does your lawyer know that you're ghouls?" I asked.

"Yes. We've retained Paul Leclerc. He has many clients in our community. He offered to represent us pro bono."

"I know Paul," I said. He was a shifter who worked with many of my patients. Vampires are snobby when it comes to shifters, but they have no choice but to use someone who can make daytime appearances in court. I'd never heard of Paul working pro bono before, however. He was the last attorney I'd ever expect to do that.

"Why do you think we can help you?" Luisa asked.

"Well, the word is that you two are friends of the community."

"Isn't Paul enough help?" I asked. "He can hire private investigators, too."

"The two of you have connections he doesn't."

Luisa and I stared at her blankly.

June gestured at the cramped store, its narrow aisles and the shelves packed with all variety of herbs, powders, potions, charms, candles, icons, and figurines. We even sold cleaning products and bug spray.

"You can access the spirit world," June said. "And you have magic."

"Last time I checked, ghosts and spells don't have a place in the legal system," I said.

"They can help you find the real murderer."

"Help" was the operative word. There aren't any spells that solve crimes. My magic advisor, the ghost of Don Mateo, doesn't know everything that happens in the material world.

"We will help you to the best of our abilities," Luisa said.

"We will?" I asked my partner.

"We will, if you can answer one question, Ms. Osman."

"Ask me."

"If you didn't kill the victims found in your backyard," Luisa asked, "what people do you eat?"

June laughed. "My goodness! I told you we don't eat people anymore. We've been vegan for years."

"How's that working out for you?" I asked.

"Never felt healthier. Eating people, particularly Americans, was terrible for my cholesterol."

Later, I wrote in an old leather-bound ledger the Friends of Cryptids had sent to the botanica after Luisa and I signed our contracts. When it arrived, I had immediately sensed magic permeating the pages. Our instructions were to use the ledger to catalog all the supernatural creatures we encountered and send photos of each creature and ledger entry to Mrs. Lupis and Mr. Lopez, who would update the Society's electronic records. I guessed the tradition of handwriting in the ledger was too important to abandon for the sake of technology.

Several pages were already full of entries from other people —those who had served in our roles before us, I assumed. The earliest entries were elegant pen-and-ink calligraphy that resembled the writing on the Declaration of Independence. Each page was filled with references to vampires, werewolves, boogeymen, and many creatures I'd never heard of. Seeing the tally of all these monsters made me shudder.

It felt momentous as I followed them with my own handwritten entries marking the sighting of three ghouls, their gender, and their approximate ages, as well as a description of a zombie named Carl. We were already well underway, following the mission of the Friends of Cryptids Society of the Americas.

MY PHONE RANG. I half expected it to be a vampire complaining about constipation but was pleased to see that it was Matt.

"The police identified the delivery driver," he said. "Benjamin Nogging of Jellyfish Beach. His company, United Parcel and Package, assigned him to that route temporarily to handle overflow."

"Yeah, my regular driver said something about a substitute driver that night. He hadn't even heard about the murder when I spoke with him."

"The police didn't just take the company's word for it. To confirm it was Nogging, they looked for a DNA match, but his DNA was not on file. But they noted he wore an unusual shoe."

"I noticed nothing unusual," I said. "Of course, when I found his remains, I was distracted by the horror of it all."

"He wore a fencing shoe."

"There's really such a thing?"

"Yeah. Fencing shoes look a lot like sneakers, but they're designed for protection and the fast foot movements fencers make," Matt explained. "The police found a sporting goods store that sold them to Nogging."

"Interesting. I wonder if fencing had anything to do with his death."

"I think if a rival fencer got him, his body would be found

full of holes from a sword. Not like he'd been eaten by an animal with only his leg left over."

I grimaced at the memory of what I had found.

"Have they done the autopsy yet?" I asked.

"Nope. I'll let you know as soon as my sources alert me."

It was a momentous day for the Jellyfish Beach Mystical Mart and Botanica. After the Friends of Cryptids bought the strip mall our store occupied, we were no longer in danger of being driven out by rising rent. It turned out the takeout-seafood joint had already accepted defeat. I arrived at the botanica to see trucks pulled up and workers removing the appliances and deep-fat fryers from the space.

"No more noxious smells of fried fish drifting into the store," Luisa said, beaming.

"No more customers buying potions to fight the food poisoning the restaurant caused," I said.

"That won't hurt our bottom line. We're taking over the space to expand our store. We can easily afford it now."

"That's awesome!"

"You can set up the new space like that store west of town that sells crystals to aging hippies."

"Why?"

"You wanted to expand our magic supplies. People like you aren't always comfortable in botanicas. It's too unfamiliar to them."

I assumed she meant Anglos like me.

"You can have books and comfy chairs and play New Age

music," she said. "You'll bring in the Wiccans and sweet old ladies from the Midwest who would be put off by the Santeria and voodoo products."

She had a good point. People from Latin America and the Caribbean were intimately familiar with the cramped, cluttered, and chaotic botanicas. North American Anglos were not, but they were comfortable shopping in artsy boutiques selling jewelry, crystals, and magic ephemera.

That didn't change the fact that we weren't in the best of neighborhoods, but I kept my mouth shut about that. Offering more magic products would be very helpful to the witches of Jellyfish Beach and surrounding Crab County. It might even serve as a gathering place to help us form a community, instead of us all practicing alone and in secret.

It also meant I didn't have to rely on the internet so much to get my supplies. The internet and unreliable delivery services.

The prospect of going on a buying spree to set up the new space was so exciting that I ignored the reek of frying oil and rotten fish that still clung to the abandoned takeout joint.

It would take tons of cleaning and witchy secrets to get rid of that stench. Perhaps a deodorizing spell would be required, like the one I use on my cats' litter box.

I've got this.

"Again, we're so sorry for your loss," Matt said to Joyce Wither, the grieving girlfriend of the late Benjamin Nogging. Her eyes were red from crying, and her flowing black hair had braided accents.

Matt and I sat on the couch across from her chair in the cramped apartment she had shared with Nogging.

I gave her a sad smile. My natural empathy, that originally drove me to become a nurse, made me want to put my hand on her shoulder. But she was wearing a purple Renaissance-era gown with lots of lace on the shoulders, and I felt weird about touching it.

"I like your dress." I realized how lame it sounded the moment I uttered it.

"The Renaissance Festival is going on now," Joyce explained. "Ben and I go every weekend, every year."

"Who wouldn't?" Matt asked. "Um, was Ben into fencing?"

"He had a fencing scholarship at his university. He was extremely talented. But once you get past the college level, there aren't many opportunities for competitive fencing, unless you make the Olympic team."

"Did he perform at the festival?"

"He was a local cast member, but not one of the professionals who travel around the country to different Ren Fests. His job at UPP paid better than that. He was a member of the Society for Anarchic Anachronism here in town, so he knew how to reenact all kinds of historical sword fighting."

"I apologize for asking the same kinds of questions the police have," Matt said. "But is there anyone you know of who had a motive to hurt Ben?"

"No. He got along well with everyone at work and at the Society. All his family members live in California. He wasn't very close to them."

"What about his friends? Or your friends? Did he have any rivals among the cast at the Renaissance Festival?"

"They all loved Ben. Why are you asking me this? The police said it looked like a wild animal attacked him."

Matt and I exchanged glances.

"I wasn't aware they believed that," he said. "We're not exactly in the wilderness here."

"They said it was most likely a gator that people had been feeding, so it associated humans with food."

My neighbor's crazy theory might be correct after all. Still, alligator attacks take place in or near water, not across the street from it. And why were the Osmans under suspicion if the police were blaming an alligator?

Matt stood and pulled a business card from his wallet.

"If you think of anyone who might have wanted to harm Ben, please call me." He handed her his card.

I stood and gave her a belated squeeze of her shoulder. "Our thoughts are with you."

When we got into Matt's truck, I asked him why the police were leaning on the Osmans if they believed an alligator killed Nogging.

"My guess is they told Joyce an alligator did it when they notified her of Nogging's death. Subsequently, they developed the theory that your neighbors did it."

"I told you I promised June Osman that I would help clear her and her sisters. Do you believe there's any chance a gator did this?"

"Not really," he said after a pause. "Especially not after you told me the Osmans are ghouls. I can't believe we have ghouls in Jellyfish Beach. I thought they all went back to New Jersey."

"These are local Florida ghouls."

"I should have known."

"What if an animal really killed Nogging," I asked, "and the bag of remains was dumped in their yard by someone who has a grudge against the Osmans? Someone who wanted to frame them for murder."

Matt shrugged as he drove out of the apartment building's parking lot.

"Seems like a real stretch to me. How would this person with a grudge be on the scene right after Nogging was killed and just happen to have a bag of remains with them?"

"The bag could have been placed there before the killing. But you're probably right," I said. "It seems more likely that whoever killed him had the remains of their other victims lying around and hadn't disposed of them yet."

"In other words, the Osmans."

CHAPTER 7
WORST PETTING ZOO EVER

June was wrong. The more I thought about it, the more I was certain Luisa and I didn't have the supernatural resources to find the murderer.

My magic had lots of awesome features. I could locate specific people, put them to sleep, and bind them. But only if I knew who the person was or had possession of an item they owned that was tied strongly to them by their psychic energy. I didn't know any spells to reveal their innocence or guilt, only a simple truth-telling spell to get them to confess.

The other thing she mentioned was that we could "access the spirit world." The only way that would help was if we could reach the ghost of the victim, and he told us who murdered him.

Luisa said she knew someone who could perform the Santeria version of a seance. I knew a couple of mediums who used other methods. However, instead of the difficult rituals allowing those of us in the living world to break through to the spirit world, I believed in taking a more direct route.

Namely, have a ghost reach out to the ghosts.

"Oh, Don Mateo!" I called out as I sat in my living room that night. "Please appear. I need your help."

I was not a medium, but I had a direct line to Don Mateo because he was attached to a grimoire of spells that I owned and, thus, to me. He was like my spiritual sidekick. I would use him to reach the delivery driver, since he was the most recently departed, and we knew more about him.

Unfortunately, Don Mateo had a fascination with my lingerie and undergarments. It must have been caused by a long-suppressed issue he had when he was alive.

One of my bras—nothing fancy, just a sports bra—came floating out of my bedroom and hung suspended in the air near my chair. Soon, Don Mateo materialized, a bra strap hanging from one ear.

"Really?"

"I apologize, madame. I honestly don't know why I arrived in your dresser drawer."

"I know why."

"How can I be of service to you?

"I need you to find the spirit of someone who was murdered."

His face fell. Don Mateo's apparition was of a fleshy man who had obviously lived well. He had a pointy beard and wore a purple tunic, green breeches, and matching hose. His wide-brimmed hat had a large feather stuck in its band, as was the fashion in Spain in the early sixteen hundreds.

"You seem concerned," I said.

"Recently murdered spirits are often in a foul mood."

"Tell him we're on his side. We're trying to find his killer."

Don Mateo harrumphed with irritation. "I'll need details about who he was."

"Benjamin Nogging. He worked for United Parcel and Package and was murdered just two houses down from here," I said. "If you want, you can see if he left any energy on a box he touched."

I pointed to the outer box of the muskrat-fur shipment that sat on my dining-room table.

Don Mateo walked over to it. Or, I should say, he floated over to it while pretending to walk.

"There's only a trace of his psychic energy on here. He simply arranged it on a shelf in the rear of the truck. He wasn't holding it when he died."

"Right. Is that helpful?"

"Perhaps. But only a little."

"If you find him, try to get him to tell you what he knows about his attacker."

"Yes, my lady."

He faded away and disappeared.

Don Mateo didn't return that night, but I trusted him to do his best to fulfill his mission.

After putting my bra away, I considered going to the garage to complete my anti-flea spell. No. I decided I would attempt some culinary magic instead.

Rather than refer to an old, dusty grimoire, I opened an old French cookbook.

Poulet en Cocotte. A chicken cooked in a Dutch oven, first on the stove and then in the oven, with pearl onions, potatoes, lardons of bacon, butter, garlic, rosemary, sage, wine, and more. Simple, traditional comfort food that, if done right, was magical in its own way.

After browning the chicken in butter, I threw in the other ingredients and put the covered pot in the oven. I poured myself a glass of what was left of the Chardonnay that I'd opened for the recipe. This would be a good time to brainstorm improvements to the botanica. So why was I thinking only about the murder investigation?

It wasn't because of the clause in our contract that said we had to help bring justice to cryptids. Yes, I wanted to help the Golden Girls and exonerate them from blame for the murder. But only if they were innocent. And I wasn't one hundred percent certain they were.

In truth, I just wanted to help solve the crime and make sure whoever did it faced the consequences.

Justice must prevail. The world must be made right again.

I was merely a humble witch and nurse—not a law enforcement officer. Why did I feel so much passion for solving this crime?

The question baffled me. Until I remembered my dream about my mother.

My mother, the evil sorceress.

She tried to kill me and was never punished. She didn't even apologize. And in the end, what did she get? My spell that cured her failing kidneys.

My mother caused the death of many people and creatures, directly or indirectly. The worst punishment she ever received was being driven from her town by its Magic Guild. She never spent a day in jail or paid any fines.

Punishing her was not my responsibility. However, thinking of her helped me understand why I was committed to finding who—or what—killed Benjamin Nogging on the Osmans' front lawn.

There would be a reckoning for this crime. No matter what.

DID YOU SEE MY EMAIL? Matt texted me in the morning.

No.

Read it. On my way to pick you up.

For what?

He never replied. I checked my email. He'd forwarded me an article from *The Palm Beach Record* about an eccentric Florida man who owned a ranch where he kept a menagerie of wild animals as pets. He ran his business as a petting zoo and was constantly getting fined for lacking permits and improperly handling his wild animals.

It just so happened that one of his "pets" escaped recently. It was a hyena.

"A hyena?" I said aloud in surprise. Hyenas were among the most vicious beasts of Africa. I'd never heard of any being owned by private collectors. It was probably illegal. And now, one of them was running around loose in South Florida?

And possibly eating delivery drivers? In my neighborhood?

Matt pulled into my driveway around 9:30 a.m. It was late for him, an early riser who often went surfing or fishing before going to work. I was still struggling to convert from working the vampire shift to having normal human hours.

I sipped my tea, waiting for Matt to come inside, but he stayed in his truck.

Let's go, he texted. *This is time sensitive.*

I sighed. "Goodbye, kitties. Don't let any hyenas in."

Bubba and Brenda looked at me with large, round eyes, as if they understood.

I hopped into the passenger seat of Matt's beat-up pickup and gave him a quick peck on the cheek. Ours was a complicated relationship. We were collaborators in solving mysteries involving both human and supernatural affairs, occasional antagonists when his role as a reporter clashed with my secrecy about my magic, and constant flirts.

I was quite fond of him: his sense of humor, green eyes, dimpled chin, and on-again, off-again beards. I didn't know if we'd ever get past the friend stage. My divorce wasn't that long ago, and I enjoyed being single. Our flirting—and his adoration of me—were all I needed right now. I mean, what could be better for an insecure witch's self-esteem than being adored?

"We're going to talk to the hyena guy?" I asked as Matt backed out of my driveway. "I thought you said it was a real stretch that a wild animal killed Nogging."

"Yeah. But now I think the hyena is a great suspect for the killing. I can't explain the bag of bones, unless your theory is correct that someone is framing your neighbors. Now, the challenge is getting the hyena's owner to tell us anything."

"What kind of person would own a hyena?"

"A nutcase. Since this is Florida, there are plenty of nutcases to go around. And with our climate, there are plenty of menageries like this."

Matt explained that in Florida, hyenas are classified as

Class II animals, meaning people can apply for a permit to own one. Cheetahs and alligators are also considered Class II, while lions and tigers are Class I and illegal for anyone except for zoos to own.

"Not that this has kept people from getting away with owning Class I animals," he added.

We drove north and then west, leaving behind the South Florida suburban sprawl, passing through farms and wetlands. During the drive, I finally told him about my career change. The moment wasn't right when we were last together, interviewing Nogging's girlfriend.

I explained about quitting my job and partnering with Luisa, thanks to the generous grant from the Friends of Cryptids Society of the Americas.

"Have you heard of them?" I asked.

"I've heard of Cryptozoology, but not that organization. Are you sure you won't be indebted to them?"

"There's nothing in the contract except for helping supernatural and mythological creatures."

"Do you even need to work anymore after getting all that money?"

"Most of it went into the business. I tucked a little away, but it's not enough to retire on."

"Hm," Matt said, as if he didn't believe me. I hoped he wasn't jealous about the grant.

On a two-lane road that probably saw very little tourist traffic, we came upon a hand-painted sign.

Doc Dewlittle's Den of Beasts and Petting Zoo.

"I would not take my kids here if I had any," I said as Matt turned into the driveway. We passed a rusted-out camper and the burned carcass of a car. A large clearing was surrounded by a double-wide trailer, a barn, and smaller outbuildings. In the center was a large pen where llamas, emus, and a donkey grazed.

As soon as we parked and got out, a portly man with a prosthetic leg approached the car.

"Good morning. That will be ten bucks apiece for admission."

"Ten bucks for what?" I muttered, but Matt handed him a twenty.

"You can pet whatever you want, except for the wolves in that building over there, the monkeys, or the alligators. And don't pet the snakes, either."

The man wore a patch over one eye, was missing an ear, and several of his fingers were mere stubs.

"Were you in the service?" Matt asked the man, nodding toward his prosthetic leg.

"No. This was Alison's work."

"Alison?"

"One of my grizzly bears. She got banished from the petting zoo after that."

"You had a grizzly bear in the petting zoo?" I asked in disbelief.

"The old girl could be quite affectionate when you rubbed her behind the jaw."

I hoped Matt didn't ask him how he lost his other body parts.

Matt introduced us and showed his press I.D.

"I wanted to talk to you about your missing hyena."

"Ricky? I'm not sad he's gone," the man said, shaking his head. "Worst pet ever."

"I didn't think hyenas could be pets," Matt said.

"I didn't either, but the guy I bought him from told me they're fine if you exercise them enough. I should have known it wasn't going to work when I took him to the obedience class at the pet store."

"It didn't go well?"

"It's the other pet owners' faults for bringing yappy little dogs there. The hyena was just defending himself. The dogs will be easy to replace."

"Has he attacked anything other than those dogs?"

"Well, their owners. And me."

"So, he does attack humans, then?"

He squinted with his one eye. "Why're you askin'?"

"How large of a range does he have? How far would he travel in search of prey?"

"In the wild, they've been known to travel fifty miles or more while hunting at night. Are you askin' because someone's been attacked?"

My neighborhood in Jellyfish Beach was less than fifty miles from here. The hyena easily could have made the journey. But I didn't want to make the man get all defensive.

"When an animal has been eaten by hyenas, is there anything about how the carcass looks that tells you a hyena did it?"

"It sure sounds like someone was eaten, and you want to blame Ricky."

"Look at these photos." Matt handed his phone to the man.

"Are you allowed to take crime-scene photos?" I asked Matt.

"They should have prevented me from doing so. Typical Jellyfish Beach Police incompetence."

"As far as I know, a carcass left behind by hyenas looks pretty much like ones left by other predators," the man said.

"Could this have been done by a tiger or wolf, too?"

"It doesn't look to me like it was done by an animal at all. Too neat and clean. Where's the rest of the carcass? And no animal would leave a nice leg untouched. Especially a hyena. They're scavengers, too."

"Oh," Matt said.

"Oh," I said.

Could the allegedly vegan ghoul sisters be the culprits after all?

"We don't really have enough evidence to guess what type of creature did this," I said. "We'll have to wait until they do the autopsy."

"Assuming we can see the results," Matt said.

"That's what you're so good at." I patted him on the shoulder.

"Thank you, sir, for your time," Matt said to the man. "We hope you get your hyena back."

"Y'all are leaving already? Don't you want to pet the llamas?"

"They look kind of mean," I said.

"They're the meanest llamas I've ever known," the man said, fingering his eye patch.

ON THE DRIVE back to town, my phone service was spotty, but I searched the internet like crazy for any reference to hyena sightings.

"I told you I already searched for that," Matt said.

"Something new could have popped up since then."

But nothing did. Next, I focused my search on the websites of animal refuges. They didn't post details, so I called them. No, they all said, they did not receive a hyena, and if they did, they would have sent it to the zoo.

I called the zoo, and they said they had no hyenas.

Okay, back to random searching. Somehow, I ended up on a site for missing and found pets. And my eye alighted upon a photo of a hyena lying on someone's couch in the Found Pets section.

Weird looking dog found in our backyard, the caption read. *Really mean. Will send him to Animal Control if no one claims him.*

Holy moly. I called the phone number.

"That strange dog you found? I think it's a hyena."

"Hyena?" The man sounded surprised, but not frightened. "I didn't know we had them in Florida."

"They're not native to Florida, thank goodness. When did you find him?"

"Three days ago."

"Thank you," I said. "I know the owner, and I'll have him call you."

After I hung up, I emailed the rescuer's number to Doc Dewlittle. I sighed.

"What's wrong?" Matt asked.

"Dead end. The hyena was found a day before the murder.

So, it couldn't have been him. And I'm pretty sure there aren't any other hyenas wandering around out there."

"This is Florida. You can never be sure of anything."

"We have to come up with a new theory," I said. "Since the sisters are ghouls, I feel like I have to help exonerate them."

"But what if they're guilty?"

"Then, I need to ensure that justice is meted out. If they attack humans, they bring attention to the supernatural community, endangering them all."

"By 'mete out justice,' do you mean making sure they go to jail?"

"That wasn't explained to me. But I doubt they want ghouls in jail where their true natures would be revealed. It's like the vampires at Squid Tower. They have their own system of punishment."

Their ultimate punishment was staking. I wondered what it would be for the ghouls, and who would administer it. I hoped I wouldn't be involved in the punishment part of meting out justice.

CHAPTER 8
FINGER SANDWICHES

When I returned home, a small envelope was taped to my front door. It contained a card with a handwritten message.

We would be honored if you would join us for tea tomorrow afternoon. RSVP with regrets only. Sincerely, the Osmans.

I had tomorrow off but didn't want to hang out with my elderly neighbors who were secretly ghouls. I mean, what did we have in common besides our neighborhood? How do you make small talk with ghouls?

And though I was working to prove they weren't murderers, I wasn't entirely sure they weren't.

Nevertheless, at the appointed time, I trudged over there with a box of assorted cookies from the bakery, vegan approved.

"Well, well, how wonderful that you could join us," said the eldest, the platinum-blonde Alex, when she answered the door. "Come on in."

She gave me a hug. She smelled of arthritis ointment and mothballs, just like you'd expect a human in her eighties to smell.

May and June sat on the couch in the living room, a silver tray holding a tea set and a matching platter with vegetarian finger sandwiches. The idea of ghouls serving finger sandwiches made me lose my appetite, even though it was definitely cucumber between the bread slices.

Again, there was nothing at all about them that suggested they were actually ghouls. Perhaps, they had remained in their human forms for so long they've lost touch with their ghoulish sides.

"We were just talking about when you first moved in," Alex said.

Was that hunger in her eyes when she looked at me? No, stop being paranoid, Missy.

"It was a long time ago. I'm surprised you remember."

"Some call us busybodies," June said, "but we just want to know what's going on with our neighbors."

"And usually, nothing is going on, with all the retirees living here," May said.

Both May and June had silver hair, unlike their eldest sister. May was the plainest looking and had a dour countenance.

"Your husband lived here in the beginning?" Alex asked.

"Yes. Before we got divorced."

"Because he became a vampire?"

I was stunned. "How did you know that?"

"Those of us in the supernatural community can spot others quite easily," May said.

"So, you kicked him out when he was turned?" Alex asked.

"He left me to be with the man who turned him," I said. "They were lovers."

All three sisters leaned forward, eager to hear about my private life.

"I had no ill will toward him," I said. "And the two of them were attacked one night by bigots. When the police came, a rogue cop staked my ex-husband. He died."

The sisters gasped and mumbled how sorry they were.

"Sadly, that is the fate of many of us in the supernatural community," June said. "It's why it's so important to keep our true identities secret."

"I know. Until just recently, I worked for Acceptance Home Care."

"Oh, they're wonderful," Alex said. "We will probably use them when we can't care for ourselves anymore."

"So, ghouls don't. . ."

"No, we don't live forever. Our lifespan is about the same as a human's. Like they say, you are what you eat."

"Don't joke like that," June said. "We're vegans now. Want a cucumber sandwich?"

She picked up the platter to offer it to me just as May was reaching for a sandwich.

May growled, a deep-throated, threatening rumble with some hissing at the end.

I jumped in my seat. Neither of May's sisters reacted. I took a sandwich and forced myself to eat it.

"Yum. Very tasty."

"Thank you, dear," Alex said.

"We can't tell you how grateful we are to you for helping to clear our names," June said.

"I'm not sure how much help I can be." I didn't mention that the ghost of Don Mateo was snooping around on their behalf.

"Something tells me your witchcraft will come in handy," June said.

"I didn't ask you how you knew I was a witch. The same way you knew my ex-husband was a vampire?"

"Partly, yes," Alex said. "That and the time you made all the garden gnomes come alive and attack people."

"Oh, yeah. It turns out that someone else put a spell on them." My mother, specifically.

"There was also the giant eel wriggling out of your home."

"That was taken care of."

"And the dragon visiting your yard."

"An old friend. I nursed him to health when he was a baby. It had nothing to do with witchcraft."

"Many strange things happen at your house, dear."

"As long as the regular humans on the block don't know about me, I'll be fine," I said.

"And as long as they don't know about us," June said.

I, of course, didn't mention that a neighbor had accused them of being cannibals. Maybe I should talk to the guy and find out why he said that.

"The best way to clear your names is to find out who the real murderer is. Do you ladies have any ideas?"

"Any sort of monster, human or supernatural, could have killed the delivery driver," Alex said. "What bothers me are the remains found in our flower garden. It was as if someone dumped them there to incriminate us."

"Who would want to do that?" I asked.

The sisters looked at each other.

"My ex-boyfriend's family?" May suggested.

Her sisters looked stricken.

"He died so very long ago," Alex said.

"Before we all became vegans," said June.

"Wait a moment," I said. "Was he . . . eaten?"

"It wasn't intentional," May said. "It was during a moment of passion."

I found it hard to associate May with the concept of passion. But it was another example, along with Mrs. Steinhauer, of how easily monsters can slip up.

"You think his family might be trying to frame you?"

"It seems like a lot of trouble to do it this way," Alex said. "It's not like they would have body parts lying around at the ready."

"I'll have my reporter friend check to see if any cemeteries were raided recently."

"Is that the cute man from the *Journal* who was here?" Alex asked.

I nodded.

"You two would make a great couple. Ah, look—she's blushing."

I was saved by the distraction of a roaring lawnmower and weed trimmer outside.

"All that noise while we're having tea? What a bother," Alex said.

A handsome man with the trimmer appeared behind the house. May rose from the couch and stood at the sliding-glass door, staring at him with her palms pressed to the glass.

That woman was too weird. Was she full of lust or hunger?

As if to answer my question, June said, "May is attracted to that young stud."

A low growl came from May's throat.

"It sounds like it's more than an attraction," I said. "It's probably a good idea if May stays inside."

"She's too old to have a fling," Alex said.

But not too old to have lawn-boy tartare, I thought.

My phone buzzed with a text. Speaking of being old, I consider it rude to respond to texts during a social visit. But the three sisters were completely focused on the lawn-mainte-nance crew, much like my cats press themselves against the window to stare at birds outside. So, I pulled out my phone. The text was from Matt.

My source at the medical examiner's office told me the bones found behind your neighbors' house were from three victims. Deaths were not recent but were within ten years. No obvious cause of death. But something gnawed on the bones. The M.E. believes a large animal killed the victims or ate their bodies after they were murdered.

"I think you're right about the bones in your petunia patch being placed there to frame you," I said.

Alex and June turned to face me again. May had followed the landscaper and now was glued to a different window.

"Testing shows the remains are not recent. Is there anyone else besides May's ex's family who would have reason to do this? What about other ghouls?"

"We don't know many other ghouls, to be honest," June said.

"There are very few living here year-round," her eldest sister said. "I'm not counting the many who come down here during winter, mainly to feed upon all the humans who come at the same time."

"Yes, I know about them."

"We spent so much of our lives forced to be in human form," June said sadly. "It's devastating when you have to hide your true nature because society is too narrow-minded to accept you."

"I understand," I said. "The murderer could be someone who found out that you're ghouls and wants to hurt you for that reason. Not necessarily for revenge, like May's ex's family. But out of hatred."

I thought again about the dumpy, middle-aged guy who said his friend called them cannibals.

"I don't see how anyone would think we're ghouls," Alex said.

May whined as she stared out the window. I jumped in my seat again.

"I would never guess you're ghouls if you hadn't told me. No way," I said.

May growled.

I added, "Please try to think of who might suspect you are."

"The plumber," May said, turning away from the window.

"When did we have a plumber come by?" June asked.

"You and Alex were out doing the tour."

"I'm sorry," I interjected. "What tour?"

"The Jellyfish Beach Historical Society Cemetery Tour. We ghouls just love cemeteries," Alex explained.

June got us back on track. "What's this about the plumber?"

"The kitchen drain was clogged," May said. "I couldn't fix it myself."

"What did you do to the plumber?" Alex asked suspiciously.

"Nothing. Perhaps I flirted with him. A bit too much."

"How old was he?"

"Oh, in his twenties, I would say."

"May, you're seventy-four!" June scolded. "That is scandalous."

"I didn't do anything wrong."

"Did you grope him?" Alex asked.

"'Grope' is too strong a word. I caressed him."

"Good grief," June muttered.

"Then I tried to kiss him."

"Heavens to Betsy!" Alex said.

"There was some kissing involved. Just a little. But something came over me. He was just so young and virile. His scent was overpowering."

"Did you assault him?" Alex asked in a whisper.

"I began to shift into my real self."

"You mean into a ghoul?" I asked.

May nodded, and her sisters looked at me like I was an idiot for asking such an obvious question.

"And he saw you?" Alex said.

"Oh boy, he sure did."

"What do you mean?"

"I almost took a bite out of him but stopped myself at the last second. He fled the house immediately. I waited for hours in a panic for the police to come, but they never did. It seemed like I could put it all behind me, but I wonder if he might try to get back at me."

"Do you remember his name?" I asked.

May shook her head. "He worked for Straight Flush Plumbing. That's all I know. Come to think of it, I never even paid him. He ran out of here so fast."

"How could you?" Alex asked.

"I'm sorry."

I cleared my throat. "Anybody want a cookie?" I held out the box I had brought. No one took up my offering. Did ghouls even eat sweets?

"Shall I put some more water on to boil?" June asked.

"Do you girls really think this young plumber would go to the trouble of killing a delivery driver and dropping off bones to get you in trouble?" I asked.

"He seemed more like the type who would come back here and shoot me," May said.

"Exactly. I think we're barking up the wrong tree. I'll see what I can find out about the plumber, but you girls need to help, too. Please ask around in the ghoul community. The old bones speak more to ghoul involvement than humans."

"Don't you know any magic spells that can help?" June asked.

"My magic must be based on something or attached to something. I don't have access to the victims' remains. Do you have anything else that could connect me with the murderer?"

"I still have the plumber's shirt," May said.

"You've got to be kidding!" June exclaimed.

"Good," I said. "And do you have the box the shoes you ordered came in?"

I figured if my package could help Don Mateo, maybe this

box that was held by the driver when he was killed would have more psychic energy on it.

"Yes," June said. "I haven't returned the shoes yet."

"Is there anything else you can think of?" I asked.

The sisters turned away from me and stared at their own feet.

Alex looked up suddenly. "I remember."

She got up and went into the kitchen, then came back with a yellow slip of paper with an adhesive strip on it.

"This was left on our door the day before when we were all out. For a package that required a signature. I don't know if it was from the same driver."

"Thank you," I said. It was unlikely that Nogging had left the note, since this wasn't his regular route, but I was so desperate for clues, I took it anyway.

CHAPTER 9

BULK-TRASH
PICKUP DAY

T uesday is bulk-trash pickup day. Before the Jellyfish
Beach garbage trucks come by, you're likely to find all
manner of things piled in people's lawns by the curb.

Yard waste is the most common: piles of dead palm fronds
and cut-up tree limbs. But you'll also find the detritus of
humanity: old cabinets from demo jobs, stained couches,
ancient TVs that even charity stores won't accept.

This morning, there was a large, dark-green plastic trash
bag in my yard. The problem was, I hadn't placed it there.

I could have ignored it until the truck came by to pluck it
from my lawn and out of my life. It bugged me, though. Why
had someone dropped their garbage on my lawn? What could
be so toxic they didn't want it on their property?

I tried to convince myself it was rubbish collected in someone's car that they simply couldn't abide anymore, so they
tossed it as they drove down my street. It just happened to land
on my property because of random luck.

Yeah, right. And it just happened to land perfectly upright at the corner of my driveway and the street.

Curiosity got the best of me. I went outside when it was still early enough that neighbors wouldn't see me rummaging through the bag. It appeared to be filled with hard objects that threatened to poke through the plastic, probably sticks or pieces of lumber.

The top was neatly tied with the red band that ran through the lip of the bag. The knot was a bit of a struggle, but I finally pulled the bag open.

It was not yard waste. Nor anything I'd ever seen before piled on anyone's lawn for bulk-trash pickup. It was bones. Human bones. Both old and new.

Yikes!

I put a wide distance between myself and the bag while I punched in Detective Shortle's number with shaking hands.

I went straight to voicemail.

"Hi, this is Missy Mindle," I said with an excessively cheery voice. "Remember me? I live on Ibis Drive where the delivery driver was killed. Well, I just found a bag of human bones in my yard. Maybe you should stop by."

The roar of a large truck came from the next block. The sanitation-department trucks were on their way. I couldn't allow them to take the bag, but I couldn't disturb evidence by dragging it away from the street, so I had to stand guard over it.

The roars grew louder. Soon, the trucks appeared, coming around the corner. The regular garbage truck that empties your bin would come later in the day. For bulk-trash pickup, the city sent a dump truck and a flatbed truck with a front-end loader mounted on top. They made their way down the block, scooping up piles of stuff and dropping them into the dump truck.

When they arrived at my house, I feared an inattentive operator would pluck me up along with the bag.

"Hey," he called down to me. "Do you mind moving out of the way?"

"Please don't take this bag," I said.

"Why not?"

"It's evidence."

"Evidence of what? Of the wasteful habits of modern society?"

"No. Of homicide. There are human bones in there." I don't know why I felt compelled to be so honest. Maybe it was his philosophical nature.

"Human bones should go in your trash bin. They're not bulk trash. You can get a ticket for that."

"Are you serious? You guys really collect human remains?"

"Not knowingly. But have you ever been to a landfill? You'll find many people in there. And creatures, I couldn't even tell you what they are. It's freaky. Have a nice day."

He honked his horn, and the two trucks moved along to the next pile of trash and Lord knows what else.

"You're certain you've never seen these bones before?" Detective Shortle asked.

"Of course I'm certain! Why would I have seen them?"

"Serial killers have been known to collect the bones of their victims."

"You think I'm a serial killer now?"

"Not necessarily. I need to consider all avenues."

"You're new at this, aren't you?"

She bristled. "I am not. I graduated from the Police Academy in Fort Lauderdale three years ago. Three years, I've been on the job."

"How long as a detective?"

"Almost a year. There haven't been many murders in Jellyfish Beach during that time."

Jellyfish Beach wasn't a good place to learn about solving murders. Once in a blue moon, we'd have a murder related to drugs, but we didn't have any gangs here, as far as I knew. All we had were some rough-looking characters who fished from the causeway. And lots of surfers with no visible means of support.

"Have you made any progress in investigating the murdered delivery driver?" I asked.

She shook her head no.

"Or the bones found in the petunia garden?"

"No." She was getting annoyed at me. "Now, with these bones in your yard, it throws a wrench into the gears."

"You mean into your assumption the Osman sisters were the culprits?"

"Yes."

"The bones in my yard prove the killer could be anyone with a car from anywhere. The killer is trying to confuse the investigation."

Shortle peered into the bag more closely. "Some of these bones look fresh, and others are old. Whoever did this has obviously been collecting a lot of them."

"Have you spoken to funeral homes? Maybe these aren't murder victims at all. They could be corpses that weren't buried. Or not cremated as intended."

"The medical examiner said the previous bones we found had signs of traumatic injuries."

"Is she certain they're not post-mortem injuries? Like from coyotes or other scavengers?"

"Not one hundred percent certain."

A theory was forming in my head. Someone wanted to harm the Osman sisters, so they planted stolen bones in their yard. The ones in the bag in my front yard were a mistake. Someone's GPS was off, and they dropped the bones in the wrong yard.

I tested my theory on Detective Shortle.

"Why would someone want to frame those elderly ladies?" she asked.

I couldn't explain that someone might know or suspect that they were ghouls.

"Oh, I don't know," I said. "A misunderstanding in the past? It's more likely than the Osmans being the murderers."

She frowned. She didn't like my theory.

"How do you explain the delivery driver?" she asked. "Would someone kill him in cold blood on the Osmans' property just to frame them? Why commit murder when all they had to do was plant the bones?"

"Because they were very, very angry about their misunderstanding?"

Shortle snorted and looked away, dismissing me, as if an older woman like me wasn't as sharp as she was.

"Maybe the bones and the murder had nothing to do with each other."

My words went unheard. She'd had enough of me, and I was sick of her. Plus, neighbors were driving by as the day began, and I didn't want them gathering in front of my house like they had at the Osmans. I went inside.

Soon, a crime scene tech came by, examined my yard, took some photos and measurements, then threw the bag of bones into the back of his SUV. I guess they didn't get the special treatment a dead body would receive.

When I left the house to drive to the botanica, everyone was gone, and my lawn was back to normal.

MY GOOD MOOD was ruined when I returned home that night to find police cars once again parked in front of the Osmans' residence. I arrived just in time to see May forced into the back seat of a patrol car before the vehicles departed.

I parked and rushed over to their house. Alex and June were sobbing hysterically. I tried to comfort them, but they were inconsolable. I put my hands on their shoulders, but quickly yanked them away. Ghoul flesh felt even colder than a vampire's.

"What happened?" I asked. "Why did they take May away?"

"They arrested her for murder," Alex said between sobs.

"Of the delivery man? But how could they prove that?"

"They didn't say," June replied. "The young detective claimed they had evidence tying his death to her. To make it even worse, they identified some of the remains from the petunia garden as belonging to a lawn-maintenance worker who disappeared a year ago. He worked for the same company that does our yard."

"Oh, my."

"The detective also said witnesses have come forward with information. But she wouldn't specify."

"Oh, my."

"Yes, we are in a pot of hot water right now. Paul Leclerc is headed to the police station to be with May when they interrogate her."

Alex looked at me with haunted, red-rimmed eyes. "Any magical help you can give us is so very much needed."

"I've been working on it," I said. "I'll double my efforts, I promise."

I spent a little more time trying to comfort them, but excused myself because I had cats to feed. Guilt weighed on me for not helping more, though I didn't know what I could do.

Don Mateo had better manifest his ghostly butt at my house soon because I was tired of waiting.

I fed Brenda and Bubba as soon as I walked in my door. And they hadn't even finished when the doorbell rang.

Not now, I thought. Who could this be?

It was Mrs. Lupis and Mr. Lopez from the Friends of Cryptids Society. They wore the same gray suits as before and looked even more grim and stone-faced than usual.

"We must have a word with you," Mrs. Lupis said.

"It is of utmost importance," added Mr. Lopez.

I knew exactly what they were going to say, and I was not wrong.

"One of the ghouls living on this street was wrongfully detained tonight," Mrs. Lupis said.

"I know. I just came back from their house."

"The Society is depending on you and your business partner to exonerate her," Mr. Lopez said. "Her sisters, too, because they are just as vulnerable."

"I think May has a few more loose screws than her sisters do. I mean, if you asked me if she was guilty. . ."

Their stern expressions gave me the hint to shut up.

"Your society seems to be pretty powerful and loaded with cash," I said. "Why are you depending on Luisa and me so much?"

"We hired an attorney for May and her sisters. However, he can't solve this on his own," Mrs. Lupis said. "This is your neighborhood, your town, your material plane. You have agency here. You must act."

Material plane?

"I'll do my best," I said. "I just hope the Osmans behave and don't make this unnecessarily difficult."

"That is beyond our control," Mr. Lopez said. "We wish you success."

They each gave me a curt nod then turned and walked away. There was no car parked in my driveway or on the street. They were like canvassers from a religious group who go door to door on foot to spread the word and pop up at yours with no warning.

And thus began the next chapter of my life. You could call it, "Ghouls."

CHAPTER 10

GHOULS

The deafening roars of a lawnmower, gasoline-powered weed trimmer, and leaf blower rocked me out of my light sleep. I glanced at the clock. 7:05 a.m. What the heck was anyone doing working on my neighbor's lawn this early?

My sleep cycle was totally messed up. After years of working the graveyard shift for my vampire patients, then transitioning to retail hours, I had a lot of sleepless nights and exhausted mornings.

To make it worse, I still did occasional patient visits. I couldn't bear to let my nursing license expire and put a permanent end to my previous career. So, I took the tests and renewed the license, allowing me to do some medical freelancing without Acceptance Home Care taking the lion's share of my fee.

Last night, I paid a visit to Agnes at her request. It turned out her problem was nothing a simple laxative couldn't solve.

But in doing so, I got home well after midnight. And now, at 7:05 a.m., I should be sleeping. Instead of listening to the leaf blower rattle my windows.

I peered through the blinds. Old Man Timmons's lawn across the street was almost done. At least these guys were fast. The logo on the truck and trailer parked on the street read "Hernandez Landscaping." The same company that did the Osmans' yard.

I was glad I didn't use them. My yard was maintained by yours truly. Yep, I cared for my lawn myself. Though I'll secretly admit I have a spell I cast twice a year that slows down the growth of the grass, meaning spending way fewer weekends sweating in the Florida heat than I would without the magic.

The leaf blower continued to roar. It seemed as loud as a dozen propeller airplanes pointed at my house. Come on, dude, enough already.

I looked across the street again. The other two members of the crew had already packed up their equipment, and the sun hadn't even crested the horizon yet.

Still, the leaf-blower guy walked along the street and Timmons's driveway, swinging the spout of the blower back and forth, spraying grass clippings in one direction and then the other.

Then he headed over to Timmons's neighbor's. In the pre-dawn light, I could just make out his silhouette against the house.

What was that? A figure moved through the shadows toward the worker. Was it a dog?

It leaped upon him. The man struggled, but if he screamed, no one could hear it above the clamor of his leaf blower.

He dropped the machine, but it continued to roar at a lower, idling pitch, while the creature dragged him across the front lawn.

As they approached the far corner of the house, the new dawn light gave me a better look.

I gasped. The creature that seized the worker was humanoid, but bent close to the ground, walking on all fours like an ape. It was naked, except for a loincloth. Its head was hairless and had eyes that glowed yellow. It held the man's shoulder in its mouth.

The creature was a ghoul. Trust me, I'd seen my fair share of them.

Frantic to save the man, I cast the quickest spell I could think of, a sleep spell, hoping to slow or stop the ghoul.

I wasn't quick enough. The ghoul dragged the man around the corner of the house and out of view.

A normal person would have called the police. Not only was I not normal, but I also knew better than to report such an incident to the authorities.

As I threw on clothes, I reasoned the ghoul was breaking the covenant to keep supernatural creatures secret, so it had no right to be protected. Still, humans ought not be involved.

I ran from my house and across the street. Was it up to me to save this man?

Racing around my neighbor's house, I entered his backyard. Beyond a narrow flat area, the grass sloped down steeply to the canal.

I saw nothing except a man's work shoe lying on the grass, a symbol of my failure to stop the ghoul.

Hurrying to the top of the slope, I scanned the water,

catching sight of the wake of something swimming quickly beneath the surface, heading down the straight waterway that intersected with another canal at the end of my street.

At first glance, you would think a gator took the lawn worker. Except for the fact that a gator took refuge on the far bank, as if it were afraid of the ghoul.

I hadn't even known ghouls could swim. But why not? This is Florida.

So where was the ghoul going with its prey? The network of canals connected with a lake where a ghoul could find a spot to have a relaxing meal. My next question was, where did the ghoul live? I'd seen no signs of ghouls living along the lake, so it must be using the waterways as travel routes. Perhaps it lived somewhere nearby.

It would be impossible for me to drive through the neighborhoods and parks that surrounded the lake, hoping to spot the ghoul emerging with its prey. Besides, they were mostly nocturnal creatures when in ghoul form, so he would hide for the rest of the day.

I caught myself. Why did I use the pronoun "he"? The ghoul could very well be a female.

It could even be a neighbor of mine.

I returned to the front of the house to speak with the rest of the landscaping crew and learn if they had seen their friend attacked. There was no sign Mr. Timmons was up, though I couldn't imagine how he slept through the racket.

When I approached the truck, I learned my sleep spell had worked after all. The two other workers lay sprawled on the grass, snoring.

"*Termine,*" I said, snapping my fingers.

Their eyes slowly opened and regarded me with aston-ishment.

"Someone abducted your other crew member," I said, hedging the truth. "The one with the leaf blower."

"What? They took him?" the weed-trimmer guy asked. "Will he be all right?"

"I'm afraid not. You need to call nine-one-one."

"The guy who uses the leaf blower is always the one people want to kill," the other one said.

MY INSTINCT WAS to call Matt, who had faced ghouls with me before.

"Oh, man," he said in a voice thick with sleep. "I don't want to fight ghouls again."

"Hopefully, we won't have to. My primary concern right now is to exonerate my neighbor."

"Wait, let me get this straight. You saw a ghoul attack a man and most likely kill him. But your first reaction is that you need to protect the ghouls?"

"I tried to save the poor man, but it happened too fast. And no, that wasn't my first reaction. My understanding is the Friends of Cryptids Society will handle the rogue ghoul. Or ghouls."

"Oh, man. Have you been corrupted by all the money they threw at you?"

"No," I said. "Well, not completely."

"You realize the attack today could point at your ghoul neighbors, right?"

"Not at all. They would never do something so rash while May is in jail."

"It's a bit too much of a coincidence, isn't it? Having two attacks on the same street?"

"Exactly. The rogue ghoul could be responsible for Nogging's death. And for the landscaper whose bones were among those in the Osmans' garden. This ghoul has a taste for landscapers."

"A ghoul would not collect his victims' bones in a leaf bag," Matt said. "Unless he's a domesticated ghoul living in human form in a house with bones piling up."

"We already discussed that the bag could have been placed there in an effort to frame the Osmans."

"But what about that bag of bones you found at *your* home?"

"A mistake. They dropped the bag at the wrong address."

"I don't know," Matt said in his most skeptical voice. "Maybe we need to worry about more than a murdered delivery driver and someone trying to frame your neighbors. I mean, there could be something dangerous going on with the ghouls of Jellyfish Beach. Man, I hate admitting we have a permanent ghoul population here."

"Something bigger going on?"

"Like a food shortage. It was awfully bold—or desperate— for the ghoul to attack the landscaper right at dawn."

"'Food shortage.' It makes them sound so innocent when you put it that way. You mean a shortage of human corpses, so now they need to go after live humans. Yuck."

"Yeah, it's hard feeling sorry for them when you put it that way."

"Well, the Osmans are sweet old . . . ghouls," I said. "Spending all their time in human form makes them more sophisticated than the creature I saw this morning. I mean, they served me tea and cucumber sandwiches."

"How charming."

"Don't be sarcastic."

The truth was, May was obviously backsliding into her more feral side. And because of this, she was sitting in the County Jail right now. Where, I reminded myself, she couldn't stay for long lest she reveal her true nature.

While I was thinking this, two police cars pulled in front of the house across the street where the landscaping truck still sat. Looks like the crew reported the missing leaf-blower guy. I truly hoped the cops wouldn't come over to ask me questions. I couldn't lie and deny seeing anything.

But I could fudge it enough to imply it had been a coyote that grabbed him, since I didn't believe there were any coyotes around here. I refused to blame it on an alligator, because then the actual gators in the canal would pay the ultimate price.

"I need your help," I said to Matt.

"I was afraid of that."

"We should find out if any bones have gone missing from cemeteries or funeral homes. That could explain where the bones in the bags came from. Including the ones from the land-scaper. And we should also search for reports of living people going missing, like what I witnessed today. That could confirm your theory that the ghouls are getting restless."

"And what if they *are* getting restless? What do we do then?"

"Stay inside and call the Friends of Cryptids."

Since Matt had unfettered access to the various newswire services and inside contacts with the police department, his assignment was to look for strange disappearances. I had the unpleasant task of cold-calling cemeteries. It did not go well.

Expecting resistance, I didn't even try calling funeral homes. I knew they would be overly protective of their clients and their own reputations. They would never admit if any dearly departed in their care took an unexpected leave of absence.

The operators of crematoriums wouldn't admit it, either. They already had enough issues with getting ashes mixed up.

Cemeteries should be different, I figured. They sold you the plot or tomb, and that was it. All they had to do was cut the grass and maintain minimal security. No one blamed them too harshly if grave-robbers came in the middle of the night. Or so I believed.

"How would we lose anyone's remains?" the irate man asked me.

"I wasn't saying you lost them. I asked if, perhaps, they were stolen."

"You think we're a bunch of amateurs? Like we don't got security cameras and such?"

"I hear about graves being robbed all the time."

"That kinda crap happens down in Miami, thanks to voodoo priests and obeah men. In old, inactive graveyards."

Really? I wondered if Luisa and I would have to deal with this at the botanica.

I asked him for recommendations on whom to call, but he hung up on me.

Next, I called a cemetery operated by the city. It was an old one, dating back to the beginning of the twentieth century, which made it ancient for South Florida. It was hidden away behind a dated middle-class neighborhood, not on a main road. I had the impression that it had reached capacity and had very little security beyond a locked gate.

I was disappointed again.

"No, we haven't had a grave robbed in over fifty years," the man said in a warm, gravelly voice. "We've had some vandalism now and then. Chickens slaughtered at a gravesite, and some tombstones with graffiti. Why are you asking?"

I broke down and admitted I was trying to account for the mysterious appearance of the bones of several people.

"Why are you searching for such a complicated reason?" he asked. "Why not go with the obvious explanation? A serial killer."

I couldn't explain that the serial killer might be my neighbor.

MATT HAD BETTER LUCK.

"Yeah, there's some weird stuff going on in Jellyfish Beach," he said.

"Like what?"

"Not just one, but two pizza-delivery people, plus four from meal-delivery apps, have disappeared while delivering food over the last couple of years."

"Were their cars broken into and the drivers dragged out?" I asked.

"No. They always were taken between their car and the customer's home, either before or after dropping off the food."

"It's really unlikely that ghouls would just happen to be hanging around in front of a home when a delivery arrives."

"I know. Maybe the restaurants' systems or the delivery apps were hacked."

"By ghouls? I'm sorry, but only the most humanized ghouls could do that, and they're very rare."

"Right. So maybe it wasn't a ghoul. Maybe it was a human serial killer."

"One of the cemetery workers mentioned that. But I saw a ghoul take a man this morning," I said.

"I'm not finished with my strange-disappearances report. There have been others that point toward ghouls. Namely, two workers at a private cemetery who were working late one night."

"Ghouls did that. Totally. It explains why the first guy I called was so defensive."

"I believe it. Last spring, an attendant on the night shift at the municipal parking garage never clocked out. They found one of his shoes lying in his booth, and he was never seen again."

"He could have been taken by ghouls," I said, "though I normally wouldn't expect them in the downtown area."

"Yeah. And you know the movie theater just north of town?"

"Sure."

"It's apparently like an all-you-can-eat buffet for ghouls. Two disappearances this year after the last screening."

"What do the police think?"

"One of them was a teenager with a history of running away, and one was a part-time janitor with a drug habit. The police don't think the disappearances are abnormal. But I noticed a telling detail. Near where some of these individuals were last seen were open sewer grates."

"Ah, that points toward ghouls."

"Also, you don't want to be loitering around convenience stores late at night."

"It's weird," I said. "Jellyfish Beach is not a big town. How could so many people go missing without a tremendous uproar?"

"Every town of every size has people disappear, and hardly anyone knows about it if the victim didn't have close ties to the community. If it's not a missing kid, or an obvious murder, it rarely makes the news. Sometimes, the missing are adults who simply move on without telling anyone. The police can't keep track of them all."

"It's creepy."

"There are a lot of monsters living in Jellyfish Beach, and no one knows about them, either. Some of them may have killed those missing humans."

"So, we really haven't learned anything useful," I lamented. "Some of the missing were probably taken by ghouls. Some by werewolves, vampires, or other monsters. And a human serial killer might be hunting along with the monsters. The cliche is that in small towns, everybody knows everybody else's business. But in small towns, there are big secrets."

CHAPTER 11
TIME FOR MY MAGIC

"I have returned," Don Mateo's voice said, coming from near my bed as I was awakening the next morning.

I heard him, but his apparition hadn't yet appeared. He gave away his location, though, by the pair of panties suspended in the air, shaped like the top of a man's head. They were mine from the top drawer of the dresser.

"Indeed, you have," I said sleepily. "Do you come with information?"

"Oh, bits and pieces, bites and morsels."

Fully awake now, I was getting impatient. "I have to get ready for work."

The visual aspect of his apparition kicked in. A genteel, though slightly buffoonish, wizard from the early seventeenth century stood beside my bed.

"Oh." He realized he was wearing my panties like a skull-cap, and they fell to the floor. "My apologies."

"Did you find the spirit of the murdered delivery driver?"

"His spirit is not bound to the earth as mine is. But the trace of psychic energy he left on the package helped me search for him. I received fragments of his spirit's emotions. A troubled soul who had a very traumatic death. He seems to be making his way to Heaven successfully, though."

"Glad to hear that, but I need to know if he gave you any details about his death."

"Oh, he was killed with a bladed weapon—an ax or a sword. He didn't specify which. And he did not tell me who killed him, nor where the rest of his body is."

"You've got to be kidding me."

"I am not. Ghosts do not make claims in jest. Nor are we very funny. I haven't met any ghosts who can tell a decent joke."

I tried to digest what Don Mateo had told me.

"Wait, you said he was killed with a sword?"

"A sword or an ax."

"Who kills people with swords nowadays?"

"I do not know, though I'd rather die that way than from a musket ball."

"Then, he was not killed by ghouls?"

"His spirit did not impart to me any memories of ghouls attacking him. No memories at all about his assailant."

"That messes up the theory we'd been developing."

"I apologize, madame. The spirit had no memory of ghouls or any such creatures."

"Unless it was a ghoul in human form," I said, half to myself. "But ghouls are much more effective killers in their natural forms. You're certain he gave no clue about the murderer?"

"He did not."

I was pleased the ghost of Mr. Nogging hadn't blamed ghouls. Hopefully, it meant the Osmans were innocent in his death, but they were not ruled out. Don Mateo's observations would be useless in convincing the police to release May. And I still had doubts about her and her sisters.

"I have two other items I would like you to sniff for psychic energy," I said.

"I am not a hound dog, my lady."

"Don't sell yourself short, dude."

I got out of bed and went into the garage where I had put the other items taken from the Osmans: the plumber's shirt, the box delivered by Nogging, and the signature-required note. I held them in front of Don Mateo's apparition.

"Do you pick up anything from these?"

"There is significant energy in this box from the spirit I spoke to. I wish you had given it to me in the first place; I could have found him much sooner. You should use the energy for a spell."

"Which spell?"

He shrugged.

"You're like my witch's familiar," I said. "You should recommend a spell, like a golfer's caddy suggests a club."

"I am a consultant. Not a familiar."

"Okay. Consult me on these items."

His ghostly hand reached out and passed right through the shirt and the yellow note.

"They belong to people who are still alive," he said. "There is no information I can glean from them. Their spirits are still within their living bodies, and I have no special access to them."

"Okay, that's fair," I said, disappointed.

"Need I remind you I am only a ghost? You are a witch and can make use of these items."

"That's my next step."

I HAVE A LOCATOR SPELL—A pretty cool one, if I do say so myself— that helps me find an individual by using a possession of theirs. It relies on the individual's psychic energy. It might help me locate the plumber using the shirt he left behind. When I called the plumbing company, they wouldn't tell me who had made the service call.

The plumber was a potential suspect, at least in my mind. Having been traumatized by May's sexual advances and attempts to eat him, he had a motive to frame her and put her behind bars. He might have killed the delivery driver or left the bag of bones. Perhaps both. I needed to speak with him to find out. I would need my spell to find him.

After work that evening, I began the spell-casting ritual. First, I drew a large circle on my kitchen's tile floor using a dry-erase marker. Next, I placed five burning tea candles along the circle's circumference at the points of an imagined pentagram inside of it.

Taking slow, deep breaths, I relaxed, cleared my mind, and put myself in a semi-hypnotic state. I focused deep inside myself, into my core at my solar plexus, and gathered my natural internal energy. All people have this energy.

Witches, however, have much more of it, and we know how to use it.

To supplement my internal energy, I drew upon the five elemental energies from the world around me: earth, water, wind, fire, and spirit. Each corresponded with a point of the pentagram. As the power surged within me, I turned my focus to the plumber's shirt.

The spell works best with objects that an owner has a great deal of affection for. A work shirt was probably not the best tool. But it was all I had, and perhaps the anxiety and negative emotions the young man experienced that day would have increased the psychic energy he left upon it.

It was a light-blue button-down embroidered with the name "Straight Flush Plumbing." It also smelled kind of funky. I reluctantly held it in my hands and recited the invocation for the spell.

The spell was in Old English, with a smattering of Latin thrown in. I didn't understand it word for word, but I knew the basic gist: "Spirit of the owner, rise up and seek the spirit from which you have been separated."

The concept was the owner's psychic energy would attempt to reunite with the main depository of the owner's energy, which was within the man himself.

Armed with the spell, I empowered the energy and forced it to manifest itself as a glowing orb that hung suspended above the shirt.

"Go find the soul to which you belong," I commanded it.

The orb floated away and passed through the wall of my kitchen.

Now came the hard part. I had to maintain a mental

connection with the orb. I cleared my mind again and allowed the images to flow into it—images collected by the orb as if it were a drone with a camera.

The orb flew from my house and down the street. I expected a long journey to its destination, then copious amounts of research with satellite maps and such to identify the plumber's location. Instead, the orb stopped at the end of my block and passed through the walls of a home.

I knew this home. It was the residence of the dumpy middle-aged man who was among the crowd gathered outside the Osman house after the murder.

The orb entered an upstairs room, a den of sorts, where a twenty-something man watched TV with his feet on an ottoman. He wore a shirt just like the one I held. He was skinny, with short hair and a paltry attempt at a beard.

The orb wanted to be absorbed into him so its energy could rejoin his spirit. But I wouldn't allow it yet. I sent the orb around the cluttered den, looking for something to help identify him, knowing the man could not see the orb.

There—on the table beside him was a paycheck stub. I sent the orb closer until I could read it.

The man's name was Jerry Diddlebum. I assumed he was the dumpy guy's son.

Mission accomplished. I freed the orb to attain its goal. Jerry twitched slightly as the orb entered his abdomen and disappeared.

I wiped away part of the magic circle, breaking the spell. After I blew out the candles, I headed straight out the door and down the block. My mind feverishly devised an excuse for why

I was about to disturb my neighbors. I decided honesty was the best means.

The dumpy, middle-aged man answered the front door. He was unshaven and wasn't wearing a very welcoming expression.

"Mr. Diddlebum, I'm Missy Mindle from down the street."

"Yeah. I know you. What's up?"

"Did you know May Osman was arrested?"

"I heard about it from my buddy, Fred, who lives behind those fruitcakes."

"I understand your son did some plumbing work for them."

"Yeah, he said the middle sister came onto him." Diddlebum laughed. "Sorry, it's not funny. But Jerry and an old lady? She's the only chick that seems interested in him."

This man was horrible. But I had to smile and be nice.

"Can I speak with Jerry?" I asked.

"Why?"

"I want to ask him some questions about the Osmans."

Diddlebum shrugged, turned toward the stairs, and shouted his son's name.

"Get your skinny butt down here. You got a visitor."

A few minutes later, Jerry came down the stairs and looked at me suspiciously.

"This is Missy," his father said. "She lives down the street. She wants to ask you some questions about the fruitcake old ladies."

Jerry's face turned pale.

"Just a few questions," I said. "Come outside with me so we can talk in private."

I wished I could add, "away from your idiot father."

Jerry followed me outside.

"I don't know the ladies," he said. "I did one service call there, and that was it."

"I heard May attacked you?"

"Yeah. I really don't like talking about it."

"Was it simply a sexual advance, or did she seem like she was going to harm you?"

He hung his head. "When I didn't let her do what she wanted, she tried to bite me."

"Bite you?"

"Yeah. And she changed into this hideous hag. And, like, I swear she had these really long, nasty, yellow teeth. They looked like animal teeth or something. I thought I was imagining it, but it freaked me out so much I just ran out of there. Left some tools behind, too, that I had to pay for with my own money."

Okay, he saw the teeth, but he didn't seem to realize she wasn't a human. Now, I would try to assess if he was vengeful.

"That must have been really frightening," I said.

"And embarrassing. So, I don't want to talk about it."

"Are you angry at her? Did you want to see her punished?"

He was surprised by my questions.

"Yeah, I guess. I mostly figured she's a crazy lady, and I told my supervisor I was never going back there. I heard she got arrested the other day."

"Yes, she did. Are you happy?"

"I guess. I mean, if she was the one who killed that UPP driver, then, yeah, she should be in jail."

It didn't sound to me like this guy had anything to do with

framing the Osmans. I could use a truth-telling spell on him, but my gut instinct told me he was being honest.

"Why are you asking me these questions?"

"Just trying to be a good neighbor to the Osmans," I replied. "Elderly people need looking after. By the way, who's their neighbor who lives behind them? Fred something?"

"Fred Furman. He's my dad's buddy."

"Thank you for your time, Jerry."

I walked down my quiet, tidy street. This wasn't an expensive new gated community, just a humble middle-class neighborhood built between the late 1940s and early '60s during one of Florida's many population explosions.

How many of the occupants of these homes, with the front porch lights and backyard swimming pools, knew Florida's growing population brought new residents who were not human?

CHAPTER 12

FURRY EARS

I walked around the corner to the next street to pay a visit to Fred Furman. He sounded like a true busybody who might have some valuable information for me.

Counting the homes from the street corner, I came to what I guessed was the one directly behind the Osman home. I stood at an angle to see into the backyard. Yeah, I recognized the house behind this one as the Osmans'. First, I took a deep breath, then walked to the front door and rang the doorbell.

I stepped back a few paces just in time. In this part of Florida, the hurricane building codes mandate exterior doors that open outward. Fred Furman flung his door open with such velocity he must have hoped to knock me into the bushes.

"I'm not going to vote for you," he said. He was a short, chubby old man with a full head of white hair and ears covered in it as well.

"I'm not a politician," I said. "I'm—"

"I don't want to join your church."

"No, Mr. Furman. I'm here to—"

"Raise money for your kid's soccer team? Nope. Not interested."

He moved to close the door, and I stepped into its path.

"Wait, let me explain—"

"And I don't want a new roof, or my trees trimmed."

He glanced nervously at the sky behind me. I needed a different tactic.

"Why do you think the Osmans are cannibals?" I blurted out.

"What?"

"Mr. Diddlebum said you thought they were cannibals."

He looked at the sky again. I turned around to see the full moon rising behind me.

"I've lived here a long time. Ever since the Osmans moved in, strange things have happened there. It was no surprise at all that old bones and a fresh body were found in their yard. Now, please excuse me. I've got to go."

His eyes darted nervously to the full moon again. I recognized the telltale twitching of his facial muscles.

"Mr. Furman, I'm a nurse whose patients include werewolves and other shifters. I don't want to bother you on a full moon, but I have questions I really need to ask you about the Osmans."

A major struggle ensued in Mr. Furman. The undeniable demand to shift to a wolf fought against his powerful urge to gossip about his neighbors.

"You can go ahead and shift," I said. "It won't bother me. But if it's okay, I still want to ask you stuff."

He glanced at the street behind me, then grabbed my arm and pulled me into the house, slamming the door shut.

Maybe this wasn't such a good idea.

"Excuse me," he said. "Nature is calling."

He left me in the foyer while he hurried through the living room and disappeared down a hallway.

Nature is calling? Did that mean he had to go to the bathroom, or shift into a wolf? Or maybe both.

Groans came from wherever he had gone. High-pitched whimpering and moaning. He must be shifting now.

Then, the toilet flushed.

The padding of feet heralded the arrival of a large white wolf coming from the hallway where Mr. Furman had gone. The wolf wore a pair of boxer shorts, either for modesty or because he hadn't been able to remove them when he shifted.

I tensed at the sight of the wolf and had to remind myself that it was only Mr. Furman. The excessive white hair on its pointy ears helped assure me.

The wolf came close enough to sniff me, making me cringe.

"Relax," he said, though the word was quite garbled, which I expected from a tongue that wasn't human anymore.

"*Fur*man? Isn't that a bit too much?" I joked, trying to relax. "A werewolf named Furman?"

I let out a nervous laugh.

He didn't care for the joke.

He stood on his hind legs, towering over me, though he was shorter than me in human form. A lot of people don't understand that werewolves don't shift into pure wolves. They're more of a hybrid. They mostly travel on four legs and can run and leap amazing distances. But they retain an opposable thumb, allowing them to climb trees. And, yes, drive a car if it came down to that. They also lack a tail for some reason.

He said something in his garbled English. It sounded like, "Osmans are fools."

"I beg your pardon?"

"The Osmans are ghouls," he repeated.

I nodded. "I know."

In a less-civilized part of the world, shifters and ghouls would be competitors for prey. But here, werewolves must shun making meals of people and limit their prey to wild game. Or eat only when in human form. The same applies to ghouls— unless they allegedly turn vegan. Otherwise, with a diet limited to people, ghouls must stick to deceased people. This becomes impossible when the ghoul population grows too large.

The short of the matter is that other supernatural creatures that might feed on people must show restraint in today's modern world. Ghouls do not, consequences be damned.

Which means Fred Furman would be no fan of ghouls. So, I had to take whatever he said with a grain of salt.

"The Golden Girls ate my pool cleaner," he managed to say with his lupine tongue.

I couldn't help but think of Gladys's erotic romances with pool boys. Except this story was a horror tale.

"Are you certain they ate him?"

"He just disappeared one day and left his truck out front. What else could have happened?"

"Are you contending that the Osmans eat people? Like I said, you told Mr. Diddlebum that they were cannibals."

"I couldn't tell the truth that they were ghouls. And yes, they eat people."

"They told me they're vegans now."

He barked out a laugh. "Tell that to the UPP delivery driver."

"What if someone else killed him? There are other ghouls in the area. In fact, I saw one take a lawn-maintenance worker just the other day."

Mr. Furman growled, and the hackles rose on his back. As you would imagine, werewolves are very territorial. Ghouls are, too, but they're also opportunistic predators.

Speaking of which.

"Mr. Furman, can you convince me a wolf didn't kill the delivery driver?"

He snarled and loomed over me, saliva dripping from his jaws. I tried to hide my fear, though my hands were visibly trembling. Monsters like Mr. Furman feed upon fear.

When it was apparent that I wouldn't cower before him, he stepped back and stopped showing his fangs.

"No, I didn't do it. That's why I dislike the Osmans," he lisped. "Their reckless behavior could get me in trouble."

"Tell me more about them."

Turning away from me, he entered the living room, jumped on the couch, and looked out the window at the moon. Then he retreated to the part of the house where he had disappeared before, his bedroom, I presumed.

I stood awkwardly in the foyer, wondering if he would come out again.

Eventually, he did. He returned in human form, wearing different clothes and disheveled white hair. Most shifters, including werewolves, can shift at will. On a full moon, werewolves have no choice but to shift to wolf. However, more experienced, powerful ones can shift back to human form after a period of time. Mr. Furman was evidently powerful.

"Okay, now I can talk more easily," he said, looking me over, assessing me human to human instead of predator to prey. "Follow me. Let's see what the Golden Girls are up to."

We crossed the living room, and he opened sliding-glass doors to a screened-in porch and pool enclosure, then exited into a small backyard. A six-foot wooden privacy fence separated the rear of his property from the Osmans'. It did not extend to the sides of this yard facing his next-door neighbors.

A half dozen holes had been bored through the wood at eye level.

"You regularly snoop on them?" I asked.

He shushed me and pressed his face against the fence, one eye peering through a hole and the other one closed. He gestured for me to do the same.

The Osmans didn't have a pool, and their yard was partly taken up by gardens. No one was outside. The inside of the house was well lit, and the blinds weren't closed over their sliding-glass doors. Alex and June sat on the couch, apparently watching a TV that wasn't visible to us.

After a few minutes of this, I grew uncomfortable peering with one eye through a hole at two people doing nothing.

"Well?" I whispered. "Nothing's going on."

"Just wait. They're always up to something."

So, I waited and watched. There is nothing more boring than watching someone else watch television. At last, something happened. June stood and walked out of view. How exciting!

In a few minutes, she returned carrying a platter of food of some sort. She placed the platter on the coffee table, and she and Alex reached for its contents.

And both began gnawing on bones.

"See!" Furman whispered gleefully.

"Those can't be human bones," I said.

"Oh yes, they are."

The bones did, in fact, look like human ribs. Both women now had smudges of red on their hands and mouths.

"This is disgusting," I whispered.

"It is. Ghouls are beasts. They need to be stopped."

I wondered who their unfortunate victim was.

After the two devoured the flesh, Alex grabbed a red-checkered paper bag and removed napkins, which she shared with June. Finally, they wiped the shocking red stains from their mouths.

Alex took small packets from the bag and each sister tore them open. Then they wiped their hands and fingers with small white cloths.

"Wait a minute," I said. "Those are moist towelettes. And that bag—I recognize it. It's from Billy Bob's Barbecue. That's barbecue sauce they're wiping up. They were eating barbecued ribs! Pork ribs, not human."

Mr. Furman looked frustrated. "We picked a bad night. Believe me, the things I've seen them do are reprehensible."

"Well, they lied to me about being vegan. That's reprehensible in some people's eyes, I guess."

I stepped back from the fence, tired of spying on the Osmans.

"I don't know, Mr. Furman. It seems like you have bad blood with the Osmans and wish them harm."

He shushed me and led me back into his house, sliding the doors shut behind us.

"I admit I don't like ghouls," he said. "They're lowly creatures, and they're going to end up getting all the monsters around here exposed. Ghouls used to be rare, but now there are too many of them in town. They took my pool guy. You saw what happened to the delivery guy. And you said you witnessed a landscaper get attacked. They must be stopped and driven out of town before it's too late."

My primary concern was exonerating May Osman, not driving ghouls out of town. But if they were threatening the anonymity of supernatural creatures, I would have to check with the Friends of Cryptids Society to see what they recommended.

After tonight, however, I had a new suspect to investigate: Fred Furman. Though I doubted a werewolf would use a sword or ax to kill prey, assuming Don Mateo's information was correct about the weapon.

Of course, Furman could have committed the murder while in human form.

Also, it was easy to imagine Furman leaving the bones on the Osmans' flower garden right after the murder to frame them. All he had to do was toss the bag of bones—that he had gnawed on—over the fence.

If so, then the second bag of bones wasn't left on my lawn by mistake. Furman must have known I was helping the Osmans. He wanted to frame me, too.

How could I prove it, though? And where did he get the bones?

I wondered if he was behind any of the mysterious disappearances around town that Matt had uncovered. If the bones were the remains of people Furman had been feeding upon, he would be in a world of hurt if the police or the Friends of Cryptids found out.

I was beginning to miss my simpler life of treating flea-ridden werewolves and constipated vampires.

CHAPTER 13
HOUSE OF HORRORS

I sat in my car, lights off, as the full moon rose higher in the sky. The front-porch light glowed at Fred Furman's house, two driveways down from me.

I had watched him leave his house, in human form, and get into his car that had been parked in his driveway. Being that it was a full moon, I figured Furman would want to take full advantage of it. Most likely, Furman had driven to a place where he could shift back into a wolf and wouldn't return for a while.

He could be frolicking innocently in the woods or hunting delivery drivers—I didn't know. If he stayed away from home for a half hour or so, I would have time to look for clues that might point to what he was up to.

Modern-day forensic science is so advanced, it's almost like magic. A century ago, detectives would never have believed that crime-scene techs could use chemicals, infrared lights, DNA, and other seemingly magical means to prove guilt.

But I came armed with real magic.

After using my telekinesis and a levitation spell to open his garage door, I set about searching for traces of blood, bone, and human tissue. A combination of two powerful spells and an amulet could find these traces and distinguish human from animal biological materials. It was just as good as CSI technology.

My eyes instantly found the scythe hanging from a nail in a stud of the unfinished interior wall of the garage. Unless you're the Grim Reaper, you probably wouldn't need a scythe to care for a suburban yard.

I lowered it from its perch and examined the blade. It was sharp but rusted. Bits of green fibers clung to the blade; he probably used it for trimming his taller palm trees.

I pulled from my pocket the felt pouch filled with a complex mixture of herbs, plants, different types of soils, my nail clip-pings, and a lock of hair from a deceased person, which I had ordered from the internet. I had imbued this amulet with the two spells, and by rubbing it on the blade of the scythe, I was assured there were no traces of human or animal blood on it.

Next, I examined the hatchet hanging on a hook nearby. It, too, had only been used on trees or shrubs.

A long, scary-looking pair of garden shears looked like they could do some serious damage, but probably not sever a limb. The magic amulet identified nothing suspicious on the tool.

There was a shovel on the concrete floor, leaning upright into a corner. The blade appeared to be sharp. This time, the amulet grew hot and vibrated in my hand. My heart quickened.

I uttered the invocation that connected me to the amulet, and images appeared in my mind. My excitement disappeared when I saw Furman had used the shovel to kill a poisonous coral snake.

Searching the garage, I found no additional dangerous tools. I even checked his chainsaw and weed trimmer, as unlikely as they would be. They were clean.

I came across a plastic garden gnome behind a bag of mulch, smiling at me in a demented way. Garden gnomes could be deadly, as I discovered a few years ago when black magic created by my mother possessed the gnomes of Jellyfish Beach. But I was certain this gnome did not kill Ben Nogging.

Wait, there in the corner—a dark-green plastic leaf bag! I rushed over to it only to find that it was filled with coconuts from one of Furman's trees.

I had no way of retracing Furman's movements over the past years to see if he was a serial killer. All I knew was that if he had thrown the bag of bones of his victims into the Osmans' yard, he would have killed them here, or brought their remains here.

Walking stooped over with the amulet just above the floor, I covered the entire garage without finding a trace of human biological matter, except for an occasional white hair from Furman's head and ears. None of his bladed tools had traces, either.

Did I dare go inside the house? Yeah, I had no choice.

I was preparing an unlocking spell when I discovered the door from the garage into the house was unlocked. Lots of people do that when you can only get into the garage using a clicker to open the automatic door. I didn't leave the garage door into my house unlocked, because I didn't park in my garage. And too many people and creatures wanted to kill me.

I stepped into Furman's empty home, my heart pounding. This was breaking and entering, in the eyes of the law. It was also idiotic when you considered a werewolf lived here.

Still, I had to be sure there were no murderous blades or bone fragments inside.

Quickly going from room to room, holding my amulet with my extended arm, I got no response from my spell. All I encountered was the horrible decor of a man who had been single for too long.

The home wasn't a man cave; it was more of a caveman cave.

Did he really need a velvet painting of dogs playing poker?

I passed through each room, receiving no sign of biological material aside from random hairs, human and wolf. Just as I was about to call it quits, I came upon a locked guest-bedroom door.

Why was the door locked? What was in here?

It was like a dark fairy tale. I imagined a room filled with the tanned hides of his victims. My unlocking spell worked quickly, and I opened the door.

To find a sight even more horrifying than tanned hides.

The room was filled with stuffed animals. Plushies, as some called them.

There were plush teddy bears, kitty cats, bunny rabbits, puppy dogs. There were ponies, ducks, frogs, piggies, and characters from every G-rated movie in the last three decades.

They covered the bed, most of the floor, an entire wall of shelves, and even the windowsills.

Furman must have taken this dark turn into kitsch long ago because it would take years to collect so many plushies.

A werewolf with a plush-animal collection? How could he look in the mirror and respect himself as a supernatural killer when his guest bedroom was overflowing with soft, cuddly toys?

Monsters aren't supposed to be obsessed with cuteness. My brain was spinning.

Until headlights swept across the window, and I realized Fred Furman was pulling into the driveway. I shot out of the room, locked the door again, and sprinted toward the garage.

When I exited the interior door, the garage door was already inching upward.

Heart pounding, I cast a quick invisibility spell and slipped under the rising garage door. His headlights blinded me, but I was confident I remained unseen. I dashed toward my car. The garage door stopped, then lowered again. Lights flashed on inside the house.

When I got into my car, the clock on my dash read 9:38 p.m. I remembered that time clearly when Matt called me near midnight with the news.

"There was another disappearance tonight," he said breathlessly. "I heard about it on my scanner."

"My neighbor, Fred Furman, went out tonight prior to shifting for the full moon. I didn't know what he had planned, but now I do. What do you know about the disappearance?"

"A Munchies Mavens driver was abducted right after dropping off a burger and fries. He recorded the delivery on his app and never arrived at his next stop. The police found his car and his phone lying on the ground at the address of his last delivery."

"Um, what time was his last delivery?"

"Let me see . . . Nine forty-two. He must have been taken as he was returning to his car."

"Drat," I said. "Furman got home just before nine thirty-eight tonight. It would be impossible for him to leave his house again and abduct the driver in that time frame."

"Okay, Furman wasn't responsible for this disappearance. It doesn't mean he's as pure as snow."

I told Matt about my search of Furman's home and its complete lack of evidence. Plus, the horrors in the guest bedroom.

"No, I don't have proof that Furman is innocent of any crime," I said. "But I have nothing at all that indicates he killed Ben Nogging or threw the bones into the Osmans' yard. I think this is a dead end."

"That's actually a good thing," Matt said, trying to cheer me up. "It's about time we narrowed down the suspects. Jellyfish Beach just has too many monsters for a small town."

That's probably the case for every town.

CHAPTER 14
JAILHOUSE ROCKED

Jellyfish Beach doesn't have its own jail. All the people the police department arrests are held at the Crab County Jail before and during their trials. The jail is in the county seat of Mullet City—named after the fish, not the haircut. But all the barbers and hairstylists in this aging agricultural city seemed to only cut hair short in the front, top, and sides, leaving it long in the back. This was true for women as well as men, based on the people we saw on the street.

I had offered to drive Alex and June to the jail to visit their sister. We were all worried about how she was holding up. Her sisters said the few collect calls May had made to them were brief and concerning.

"Why do they call this hairstyle a mullet?" Alex asked as we sat at a red light watching a man with a particularly egregious one walk by.

"I don't know. It supposedly means 'business up front, and

party in the back.' It was popular back in the eighties and nineties."

"No one has their hair like this in Jellyfish Beach," June said.

"I guess we're too hip and cosmopolitan for that," I said. Actually, it was because the average age of our residents was over seventy.

Entering the jail was an intimidating process, going through metal detectors and wand frisking. The other visitors had an air of desperation. We probably did, too. It's not a happy experience to have a relative or friend incarcerated. Some say the inmates are people who failed at being part of society, but I could argue many are those who were failed by society.

The visitation room was like the ones you see in movies, with cubicles on either side of a thick plexiglass window and old-fashioned phone handsets to speak through. Alex and June sat in chairs near the glass while I stood behind them. I was here mainly for emotional support. Though, I secretly had a feeling of guilt that I had not done enough yet to help clear May.

Sitting in the cubicle to our right was a mother with a young boy. On the other side of the window from them was an older female inmate. To our left was a middle-aged man speaking with a woman who was around his age.

A male guard stood at the rear of the prisoners' side of the room. A second guard, a woman, led prisoners into the room one by one to the appropriate cubicle to meet their waiting visitors. In this wing of the jail, all the prisoners were women.

May entered, looked haggard and numb. After she sat down behind the glass, I averted my eyes while the three sisters cried and spoke among themselves. It was awkward, believe me.

I wished I had my phone with me, but it was not allowed. Before we arrived, I got a text from Matt with the news from the medical examiner's office that the delivery driver's leg had been cleanly severed by a metal tool, such as a sword or ax. This confirmed what Don Mateo told me.

To me, it meant it was highly unlikely a ghoul did it. This didn't help May in the eyes of law enforcement because they didn't know she was a ghoul. In their eyes, the woman in her seventies could conceivably wield a sword or ax. I doubted she had the strength to do so. Unless she was in ghoul form, and in that case, she didn't need to use a weapon.

As far as I knew, no ax, sword, or any such weapon was found at the Osmans' home. But my only source for that information was Matt, and he had to rely on his limited access to the police department. I would never know for sure until the case went to trial.

When the conversation between the sisters slowed, I decided to insert myself. Alex and June had already asked May questions about her welfare, so I just jumped straight to the point.

June allowed me to use her phone handset.

"May, I learned only minutes ago that a sword or ax was used on the delivery driver. That's good news because it means the killing wasn't a . . ." I glanced around at the other cubicles and lowered my voice. "It wasn't an act of feeding on prey."

Instead of being happy, the three sisters looked at me with horror.

"What's wrong? Did I say something bad?"

"Iron," June whispered. "It's true."

"What do you mean?" I asked.

129

"We sensed the presence of iron in our front yard that night," May said over the phone.

"Weapons made from iron—not steel, but pure iron—are the most lethal threats to ghouls," Alex said.

I glanced around nervously, but all the other visitors were too engrossed in their interactions to hear us.

"This has been the case since ancient times," Alex continued, "when bronze swords were abandoned for iron. Humans almost wiped ghouls off the face of the earth. And when steel came along, they were not as deadly."

"Thank heavens they don't make weapons from iron anymore," June said.

"Except for the one we sensed in our yard that night."

"Wait a minute," I said. "If someone came to your house carrying an iron weapon, it would be to kill one or all of you. Why was a human killed instead?"

"Because the delivery man interrupted the attack," June said. "He saw the attacker coming to our door with the weapon, and it was obvious he was up to no good. So, the poor delivery man had to die."

"And then the attacker escaped," June said.

"There's still no explanation for where the rest of his body went," I said and was completely ignored.

"That means the ghoul slayer is still out there," May said ominously.

"Who would try to kill ghouls?" I asked. "And who would know about this power of iron? Or that you guys are ghouls?"

The sisters looked at each other, then at me with anxious faces.

"No idea," June said.

"I can't bear being in here and not with you two when you're in danger," May said through the handset. I returned it to June.

"You're safe in here, dear," she said.

"But *you're* not!" May said. Her volume was loud enough that I could hear her with the handset against June's ear.

"We'll be fine," June insisted.

"What if he's a Paladin?"

"What's that?" I asked.

"A religious cult whose mission is killing monsters," Alex said. "But they haven't been active in hundreds of years."

"You girls are older than I thought," I said.

"We're not that old! I read about the Paladins."

"What matters is we must stick together," May said.

"I'll keep an eye on your sisters," I said near the handset. "And I'm sure the Friends of Cryptids will help us protect you."

"Who is that?" June asked me.

"Long story. Just know that you've got an organization with lots of money and resources looking out for you."

"Can they get me out of here?" May asked.

"They're paying for your lawyer," I said.

"He said he was representing us pro bono," June said.

"He wouldn't be the first lawyer to be full of it."

The answer didn't seem good enough for May. Her eyes darted about anxiously, as if she were having an episode of claustrophobia.

The lights blinked in the room. Visiting time was over. Crying and words of endearment came from the cubicles around us as loved ones said goodbye. The guards began escorting the prisoners to the door at the rear of the prisoners' side of the room.

"Keep the faith," I said to May. "We'll find the actual murderer and get you out of here."

Alex and June wiped away tears and pressed their hands against the glass opposite May's hands.

May shook her head. "I can't stay in here while a ghoul slayer stalks you."

"We'll be fine," Alex said.

The female guard tapped May on the shoulder. When May didn't respond, the guard grabbed her by the upper arm and pulled her gently, but forcibly, to her feet.

May gave one last forlorn look at us as she went through the doorway.

And then, the world went nuts.

The high-pitched scream of an animal came from behind the door. It sounded like a giant rodent. Human screams, female and male, followed, along with an eerie mewing. Clattering and thudding erupted behind the door as large objects hit the walls.

The sisters exchanged knowing, worried looks.

The door at the rear of the room burst open. A giant ghoul stood in the doorway.

"May, no!" Alex shouted.

This creature did not look like May, except for the silver hue of the tufts of hair on the top of her head and covering her privates. Tall, bony, gray-fleshed, and naked, the creature was horrifying. She had long arms with sharp, curved claws. Her eyes were yellow orbs sunk deep in dark cavities in her skull, above a nose that was nothing but two slits. Her mouth had a powerful, distended jaw which opened to reveal yellow, dagger-like teeth and powerful molars behind them for crushing bones.

"Mommy, is that Uncle Bill?" the young boy to our right asked.

"No, even Uncle Bill isn't that ugly," his mother replied. "I believe that's a member of the Florida Legislature."

"It's a monster!" the older woman on our far right screamed.

"Run!" shouted the man to our left.

The monster—I mean, May—charged at the plexiglass window. She flung her body into it, causing it to shudder and bow inward from the powerful force. She was impossibly strong.

The two guards rushed back in. The woman sprayed May with pepper spray. She backhanded the guard and sent her flying into the wall. The male guard shot her with a Taser. May plucked the dart-tipped wires from her back, picked up the guard, and threw him at the window. He bounced off and landed unconscious on the floor.

May made another attempt to crash through the plexiglass. She hit it with such force that I was sure it was going to break. It didn't.

Three large male guards rushed into the room.

One took his first look at her, screamed, and ran out.

The other two attempted to tackle her. It did not go well for them. I didn't know a human body could penetrate a wall so easily, but I do now. The other guard vaulted through the open door, landing with the loud crash of splintered wood.

I wondered if May should flee through the rear door, but

figured her best route to the outside world was through the visitors' entrance. If she could only get through the plexiglass.

Moral quandary: do I cast a spell to help her do so? Or was it wrong to take part in something illegal?

More guards crowded into the room, brandishing weapons. Two fired pistols at May. Another aimed a shotgun.

According to the Friends of Cryptids' mission, I must help the ghoul escape scrutiny by humans.

I quickly cast the spell. Intense heat radiated from the plexiglass. All the visitors in the room had fled by now except for the sisters and me, but we had to retreat from the window because of the extreme heat.

The bullets did not seem to bother May too much, and the wounds appeared to be healing. But I didn't have confidence she could survive sustained barrages of fire.

"Can bullets kill ghouls?" I asked the sisters.

"I don't know," June said.

"One or two won't," said Alex. "But if her body is damaged beyond a certain point, it can't regenerate."

I fed more energy into my spell. The window appeared to be melting somewhat. My view of the other side was getting blurry.

May threw a guard at the window. He screamed as his clothing burned, and the window bulged inward, but he didn't come through.

The spell, though, was having its effect. Another round of shots echoed in the room. The retorts were much louder now, which meant the window was less solid.

As her wounds healed, May must have realized her time

was running out. She turned toward us, and my eyes met her feral glowing orbs.

She charged the glass on all fours, sprinting like a chimpanzee. She leaped.

And she passed through the molten glass, landing behind us.

She nodded to her sisters, then left the room through the door we had used. Screams came from the hallway along with the shattering of glass. An alarm sounded.

And May was gone.

"I thought ghouls only came out in their true form at night," I said.

"We hunt at night," Alex replied. "Ghouls will be ghouls whenever we want."

"Where will she go?" I asked.

"She's smart enough not to return to our home. She'll go where she can find food and hide until we find a way to exonerate her."

I imagined she'd go to a cemetery. Or, if she wanted a ready supply of humans, to a shopping mall. In any event, this was not a good development.

I got my phone back at the visitors' check-in, and we left the jail while the facility was in such confusion, they didn't have the chance to detain us for questioning. Miraculously, I drove us safely from the grounds just before the complex went into full lockdown.

As soon as we cleared the gate, I called Matt.

"She escaped? A seventy-year-old woman?"

"Seventy-four," I said. "She did it in ghoul form."

"Uh-oh."

"Exactly. In front of tons of witnesses. So much for keeping ghouls secret."

Alex, who was riding shotgun, tapped me on the arm.

"Old and wise ghouls such as ourselves have a little trick," she said. "We can project to anyone viewing us an image of ourselves in human form, even when we're in our natural state."

"You mean what the guards saw was a seventy-four-year-old woman kicking their butts?"

Alex nodded. "I'm sure May was smart enough to cloud their minds. The visitors on our side of the glass saw the real May, unfortunately."

"What about the security cameras?"

"The cameras in the room with her would be clouded, as well. I can't say the same for all the cameras she may have passed on her way out of the jail."

"Did you hear that, Matt?" I asked.

"Yeah. That's remarkable."

"Please do all you can to find out if word spreads throughout law enforcement about a ghoul or gets into the news."

"Will do. You realize there's nothing we can do if it does, right?"

"Yeah. But we need to know what we're dealing with. And there's another task I'm going to assign you."

"Come on, Missy. I have enough assignments here at the paper already. I need to leave in a moment to cover a city council meeting about sewage treatment."

"What could be more important than that?"

"This town produces more sewage than you'd like to know. But, okay, what else do you want?"

"How common are iron weapons, like swords? And who collects them? We must look into this. And it's a more pleasant topic than sewage."

I caught a view of June's face in my rearview mirror. Her expression was dark and grim.

"You don't really think the guy with the iron weapon was from that Paladin cult, do you?" I asked her. "It could just be some weirdo who likes to make replica swords."

"But why from iron and not steel?" June said. "Pure iron isn't used anymore for weapons. And the effect it has upon ghouls is not common knowledge."

"I understand."

The truth was, I wasn't so worried about a guy killing ghouls. I wanted to find the guy who killed the delivery driver so we could exonerate May.

And we needed Paul Leclerc to clean up the legal mess she created by escaping from jail.

CHAPTER 15
FESTIVAL FOLLIES

Matt and I met for breakfast at a cafe across from the beach. It was a longstanding ritual for us, having originated when I worked nights. I would meet him after I finished my overnight vampire patient visits and before he headed into the newsroom.

Now, we could meet in similar circumstances—as we both began our days.

Living separately, of course.

These breakfasts used to be about collaboration. And friendship. That was all, as far as I was concerned. Matt was a different story. It turned out he'd had a crush on me the entire time.

However, having gone through a divorce and losing my ex-husband to the stake had hardened me. So had my work: the rollercoaster of emotions in the ICU. And after I quit, so had the mind-boggling revelations as a home-health nurse encountering supernatural creatures and monsters that shouldn't exist. Both jobs had built a protective crust around me.

I was like the earth: the fiery miasma of my heart was encased in miles of rock.

Still, over the years, my friendship with Matt had grown. I came to enjoy, then cherish, our time together. A portion of the rock surrounding my heart fell away.

Still, I couldn't fall in love. Not yet. Maybe never.

Matt confessed his feelings to me. We kissed occasionally and shared the warmth of embracing.

I offered to escalate our relationship from platonic to intimate. But not to fall in love. A friends-with-benefits arrangement. That, I thought, was the perfect situation all men craved.

Not Matt. He wanted more. He wanted the stone-encased heart I could not offer him, even to the point of declining my offer.

He wanted to share my bed only as a committed lover. Perhaps as my husband.

So, that's the backstory of our breakfasts. They used to have an undercurrent of Matt pouting that he could only have breakfasts with me, never proper dates. They were working breakfasts, to be clear—hardly even social events.

And now, here we were again. Meeting for breakfast to discuss our investigations into weird supernatural events. I've always had a personal stake in this work. Matt did it out of curiosity, out of a fascination with the occult and macabre.

As a reporter, he gave up opportunities to break earth-shattering news about folklore that turned out to be real. Because we had a deal that I would share the crazy things I learned with him if he kept them secret.

He knew that as amazing as the scoops could have been for him, they also could have pushed him from the realm of serious news into too-impossible-to-believe tabloid territory. That was part of the reason he was cautious and honored our deal.

But I had to admit that he gave up the chance for fame, however fleeting, for a more basic reason.

His feelings for me.

This cute, skinny guy, with growing streaks of gray in his shaggy brown hair, was precious to me. My great friend, and someday, perhaps, something more, was a treasure.

I took advantage of him and rode him like a mule when I tried to solve mysteries. You're pushing him too far, I told myself. Yet, here I was again, having breakfast at the beach, him with his usual omelet and me with my crepes.

And him still sticking with me despite it all.

Don't mess this up, Missy.

"Morning." I kissed his bearded cheek. "Did you learn anything?"

I obviously had learned nothing myself, as I milked him for information once again.

"As far as I can see, there's been no mention of any sort of monster in the jail break. The official word is that May Osman slipped out during visiting hours. My contacts at the Sheriff's Office and the County Jail admit some guards were injured, but they won't even admit an elderly prisoner did it. There's definitely a cover-up going on, probably out of embarrassment. Whoever knows the truth is staying silent."

"What about the security cameras?"

"I asked about that. The footage reveals nothing. Some of it might have been mysteriously deleted."

"Ah," I said sipping my tea, "how convenient."

"Convenient for everyone. Let's face it. This is one story in which I don't mind being stonewalled."

"There's been a police car parked on my street near the Osman home ever since this happened."

"Law enforcement is looking foolish. They're going to put everything they have into finding her."

I watched Matt devour his omelet as if he were under a deadline to finish it.

"We need to find a guy with an iron sword or ax," I said.

"I did a little research on that. Pure-iron weapons were going out of fashion before the Roman Empire. You only find them in museums and rare personal collections. This weapon, if it exists, was probably made in contemporary times by a sword-maker for hobbyists."

"Okay."

"There are a lot of sword smiths on the internet, but the ones I found made their blades with carbonized steel. That's the best material. So, the bad guy probably had to custom order his sword. Or get it made by an iron-working blacksmith."

"If he went to all this trouble, it was for a reason," I said. "He wanted iron because he knows the effect iron has on ghouls."

"How would he know that? It's not common knowledge. I've never come across that fact in the research I've done on ghouls."

"The girls think he's part of a monster-hunting cult coming after them. The delivery driver was simply collateral damage."

"I see." Matt gulped his coffee. "This case sounds like it will need a lot of tedious work to trace where the sword came from and who bought it. I'll help you as much as I can, but I have to put my newspaper job first."

"I know. You have a story about sewage to write."

"I do." He wiped his mouth with a napkin. "And it's due today for tomorrow's edition."

I grabbed the check when it came. "I'll get this. Thanks for your help. I truly appreciate it. How about getting together this weekend?"

His face lit up. "You mean for a date?" His expression darkened. "Or for investigation?"

"A little of both. I just remembered the Renaissance Festival is going on. Don't they usually have artisans selling swords and stuff?"

"I guess."

"And remember, Ben Nogging was a cast member there. Maybe we'll find some leads."

"I haven't been to the festival in years."

"Then it will be fun. We'll drink some ale and eat giant turkey drumsticks and shop for ghoul-slaying swords. Let's go Saturday."

"I'll pencil you in."

Matt got up to leave, then bent down to kiss me on the cheek. I moved my face, so he caught me on the lips. It was a quick kiss, but it left me tingling.

He smiled. "What a pleasant way to begin my day."

THE RENAISSANCE FESTIVAL took place over several weekends every year in an enormous park about a half hour south of

Jellyfish Beach. Living in a town filled with retired seniors, it was refreshing to see the wide slice of life that showed up. There was everything from families to young kids to young adults who were hardcore cosplayers—decked out in bodices and flowing skirts, as well as cloaks and swords. In fact, there were folks in all sorts of costumes, some having nothing to do with the Renaissance or Middle Ages.

Matt griped about the long lines at a security checkpoint.

"They're scanning everyone for firearms," he said. "That's good. But they're letting this guy in?"

He gestured toward a tall man in a Viking costume with a battle axe in his belt.

"And that guy?"

The middle-aged guy in the next line wore chain-mail armor and had a two-handed broadsword strapped to his back.

"The blades are probably dull," I said.

"Doesn't make me feel any better."

And that was just the attendees. The performers and vendors who worked here, many of whom lived in encampments, were a sight to behold.

Funny how, in a world that professed to disbelieve in magic and monsters, there were so many people who lived rich fantasy lives.

I wanted to make this day as fun as possible before we began asking questions, so I fulfilled the promise of ale and food. We watched an authentic Renaissance music troupe, then a rowdy Celtic party band. Then it was on to watch a jousting tournament.

Finally, we found a sword-fighting demonstration in a small clearing surrounded by palmetto trees. A banner tied to the trees had the logo of the local shire of the Society for Anar-chic Anachronism. We watched five men and one woman, in various styles of armor, duel each other with different types of swords. A second woman explained to the audience the different weapons and fencing techniques.

When it ended, Matt made a beeline to the announcer.

"My condolences for losing Ben," he said.

The woman, in her thirties, was taken off guard.

"He was killed in my neighborhood," I explained. "With a sword or ax."

Now, the woman was really confused.

"I heard he died in a robbery of his truck," she said.

I shook my head. "It wasn't a robbery. Do you know of anyone who had a beef with him?"

"Everyone in our group loved Ben," she said.

"What about other groups?"

"He had no enemies, as far as I know. But there are some rough characters here who are attracted to weapons and brute force."

"Do you know if anyone has an iron sword or ax?" Matt asked.

"No one in our group. You should ask the armorers." She pointed to the market booths that hugged the paths nearby.

We thanked her and headed in that direction. On the way, we went down a windy path in the shade of oak and gumbo limbo trees. We passed encampments of sorts. One looked like a military camp and appeared as if it were more for show than function.

A second camp looked like people were actually living here during the run of the festival. The tents and campfires were actively used. Coolers were partially concealed out of view in the rear. Weapons and armor hung everywhere.

A banner flapped in the breeze, bearing a coat-of-arms and the name, "The Knights Simplar."

Unlike the first fake camp, the military re-enactors hanging out here were not friendly. They lounged about, drinking ale, and sharpening the blades of their weapons, giving surly looks at the fair-goers who walked by.

"'Tis a witch!" a re-enactor shouted in a poor attempt at an English accent.

I turned in his direction. He was pointing at me.

"Aye, she's a witch," said another.

"Don't worry," Matt said. "They're just doing a skit. They probably do it all day long."

He might be right, but it made me uncomfortable, because I *am* a witch.

"She's Satan's minion for sure," said the first man. He wore a tunic, breeches, and a floppy wide-brimmed hat. Tall and stooped, he walked alongside me, his sharpened dagger still in hand.

"It's not a joke," he said to me in a low voice. "We know what you are."

"Okay, you've made your point," Matt said. "Go pick on someone else. Missy, let's keep walking."

A short, stout man was also following us now. We'd passed the border of their encampment, but the two re-enactors remained behind us along the path.

"She's a witch," the first man announced to the fair-goers behind me. He pointed at me dramatically. "The stench of evil pervades the lass."

A group of teenagers walking the other way giggled.

"Come on guys, knock it off," Matt said.

"Just ignore them," I said. "They can't do anything to us, or they'll be kicked out."

I considered tossing a spell at them, a stink bomb perhaps. But that would draw too much attention.

We finally reached the area of vendor booths, and the crowd got busier. The bothersome men seemed to have retreated.

Booths selling jewelry, artwork, period clothing, and faerie-themed accessories abounded. Finally, we came upon what we sought.

"The Dark Blade Armory," read the sign.

This booth was well appointed, with wooden walls upon which hung swords, daggers, and battle-axes. A handful of pikes stood in the corner. Inside a display case were smaller knives with fancy jeweled hilts.

A man with the leather apron of a blacksmith greeted us as we stared at the variety of weapons. The swords ranged from single- and double-handled medieval broadswords, Roman-style swords, scimitars, and Samurai swords. There were also rapiers and modern cavalry swords. The craftsmanship was superb.

"Do you sell iron swords?" Matt asked the man.

"Iron? No, we use only steel for strength and durability."

"If I wanted an iron sword, where could I find one?"

"Why would you want an iron sword? They're inferior—more likely to bend."

We couldn't say we wanted iron for its ghoul-killing properties.

"A gift for a friend who's a collector," I lied. "He's really into the history of the Iron Age."

The armorer frowned. "Let me think. I believe there's a guy who makes obscure stuff like that. Iron swords, even bronze swords. I met him at another festival. Hang on."

He went behind the counter and pulled out a notebook filled with business cards. "Oh, yes. He's local, too."

He copied down the information on a piece of paper and handed it to me.

"Does anyone at the festival have an iron sword?"

"Not that I know of. Can I interest you in the wonderful quality of high-carbon steel?" He gestured at the walls of weapons.

Out of curiosity, I took down a medieval-style sword. It was a size I could handle, not one of the big ones that you'd need to be a muscleman to swing.

The sword was lighter than I'd imagined. It was well-balanced and felt good in my hand. I tested the edges of the blades with my thumb. They were sharp, but not dangerously so.

"Like it?" Matt asked. "You do need a new sword. Your old ones are so out of style," he said sarcastically.

I'd come across magic spells in various grimoires that called for swords to be used ritually. I didn't need a sword. But for some reason, I wanted this one.

"How much?" I asked.

"Two hundred and fifty," the man said. "Take it now, and I'll give you ten percent off."

"Ah, there she is—the witch!"

The two bothersome men were back.

"Do you know them?" Matt asked the armorer.

"They're part of the make-believe crew. The re-enactors who take things a little too far. I stay away from them, especially when they've been drinking. Which is most of the time."

"What would a witch want with a sword?" asked the second man, the stout guy with a big scar on his cheek. Probably from a re-enactment gone wrong.

"Leave me alone, or you'll find out," I said.

Both men drew their blades. The first one had the dagger, the stout one had a sword like mine.

"We actually know how to use our weapons," the first man said. "We train with them regularly."

"Good for you. I have a real job. I don't have time to play make-believe."

This angered them, and they moved into the booth with me. I faced them with my sword at waist level. The point was aimed at them, but not in a menacing way.

The postures they took, and the way they held their blades, were menacing.

A crowd began to gather, evidently believing this was a performance.

"I'm serious about you being a witch," the first man said in a low, dark voice. "And I think the world needs to be rid of witches."

"Like you're going to kill me at a Renaissance festival?"

His eyes said he was seriously considering it.

Instinctively, without thinking, I whispered a brief incantation.

My sword glowed bright yellow and red, as if it had just been pulled from a forge.

The crowd gasped. The two men stepped back. Their faces showed shock and fear.

I moved toward the first man. He backed away further.

"Knock it off before anyone gets hurt," the armorer said. "I'm calling security,"

I twitched my glowing sword, and the men's dagger and sword glowed, as well. They screamed in pain and dropped their weapons.

"You burned my hand!" the stout swordsman cried.

"Get away from me now," I said. "I don't want to ever see you again."

They melted away into the throng that passed along the path. The glow disappeared from the sword, and the small audience applauded.

"I'll take it," I told the armorer. "If you throw in a scabbard."

"You got it."

CHAPTER 16
ARMS AND THE MAN

"I want to find out more about those creepy thugs," I said, while the armorer packed my sword into a long cardboard box.

"The banner at their camp said they're the Knights Simplar," Matt said. "Whatever that means."

"They're a bunch of losers," said a woman in a tight corset, with lots of cleavage. I recognized her as part of a comedy troupe of women who made double-entendre jokes and threw mud at each other. She still had traces of dirt on her cheeks from her last show.

"Do you know anything about them?" I asked her.

"Most of them are just local yokels," she said, tugging on her left pigtail. "There's like three of them who are really hard-core. You met two of them. The three of them travel around the country to all the Renaissance festivals. I've seen them at ComicCon and many other conventions. Anywhere there's cosplay going on, these guys show up."

"So not just historical stuff?"

"Nope. Science fiction and, even, Furry cons."

Yes, hardcore indeed, I thought, but I didn't voice it. It sounded as if this woman also went to her share of events like this.

"Why are they so menacing?" Matt asked.

The woman twirled her finger around her temple. "They're nuts."

"I can see that," Matt said. "But what are they really after?"

"You saw them—they accused her of being a witch. That's what they do. They come here and claim they see actual witches, faeries, and elves. They go to science fiction cons and claim they see real aliens and Lizard People."

"They don't understand it's dress-up, role-playing fun?" I asked.

"The scary thing is, they *do* understand. But they believe all the role-playing attracts the actual creatures and monsters."

"Are these guys violent?"

"One time, I saw them attack a guy in a Bigfoot costume."

"Was it really Bigfoot?" Matt joked.

"No. It was a dentist from Memphis. I think he sued them. Anyway, I've got to run. Our next show is in fifteen minutes."

We thanked her as she dashed off.

"Ready to head home?" Matt asked me.

"I want to find out a little more about these nuts," I said.

"I think it's best to avoid the nut encampment."

"Agreed. Let's see if there's an information booth."

Sure enough, near the entrance to the festival was a tent that appeared to be the headquarters of the operation. In an office-like space in the back, a woman at a desk argued with a man dressed like King Henry VIII.

In the front were tables with books and souvenirs for sale, plus brochures. I picked up a pamphlet that had background information on the professional actors who made a living working at Renaissance and pirate festivals throughout the country in the warm-weather months. The festivals hark back to the days of traveling circuses and carnivals.

I flipped through the pamphlet, hoping there was a listing for the Knights Simplar.

"Minced-meat pies were in my freaking contract!" King Henry VIII practically shouted at the woman behind the desk. "I'm tired of eating turkey legs!"

"Bob, when guests see King Henry the Eighth, they want to see him eating a giant turkey leg."

"But that's such a cliché! King Henry ate minced-meat pies, too. I love them."

"Our local food vendors don't sell them."

"That is a travesty," he said, sweeping his cloak with his arm in a Shakespearean gesture. "Why are they selling hotdogs and chicken tenders if this is the sixteenth century?"

"That's what families with kids like to eat. Now, please go get a turkey leg. The Royal Procession is starting soon."

"Next, you'll be expecting me to walk around with cotton candy."

"Please be reasonable."

"I should just quit right now."

"Listen, Bob, South Florida is full of fat guys with beards and jowls. And the company has other Tudor king costumes. If you walk out of here, we can replace you before you even reach the parking lot, and you'll never get another King Henry gig again."

The king slumped, defeated.

"Now, grab your turkey leg, and don't get grease all over your face."

I looked away as he slinked from the tent with the opposite of a royal bearing.

"Be sure to wave at the children," the woman called after him.

Flipping through the pamphlet, I finally found the page I was looking for.

There was an illustration of the Knights Simplar's banner that featured a symbol of a dead dragon. Odd, I thought. The text was a mess of flowery prose about chivalry, knights, and maidens in distress. The order's leader was a Lord Arseton. But what I found chilling was the order's mission: "to hunt and destroy evil creatures in our midst, whether it be dragons, demons, witches, or heretics."

The mission might sound childishly grandiose to the typical person but what you'd expect for the fictional role this group was playing.

However, I knew the creatures they hunted were real. Especially me—a witch.

I showed it to Matt. "Rather serious for a bunch of folks who like to wear costumes and drink ale, wouldn't you think? There was something sinister about the guys who accosted me."

"Yeah, they've gone off the rails."

We made our way back to the armorer's tent via a path that didn't pass the Knights Simplar's encampment. Music broke out ahead of us, with fifes, recorders, and tambourines. The Royal Procession was headed our way, and we had to step aside to let them pass.

Leading the procession was King Henry VIII and a not-yet-executed wife. She rested her hand on his. In his other hand was a giant turkey leg, already missing several bites. He waved the leg at the crowd and smiled, his lips covered with grease and his cheeks filled to bursting with turkey.

It turned out that Henry didn't mind turkey legs after all.

After the knights, jesters, ladies-in-waiting, and other characters passed, we continued on our way. I picked up my boxed sword, and we left the festival. I'd had enough of Renaissance fun and modern insanity.

While I drove us back to Jellyfish Beach, Matt was glued to his phone, searching for information on the Knights Simplar.

"I've found a few references to them on the sites of other festivals, but can't find anything substantive," he complained. "You'd think a quasi-religious order of knights would have a website, right?"

"Try searching for Lord Arseton."

"Okay. Yes, he has a website. And it's weird."

"In what way?" I asked.

"It's very text heavy. Like, it seems to be a bunch of manifestos."

I glanced at Matt's phone. The site looked like a Bible.

"Great. Sounds like a future mass shooter, except he favors bladed weapons. What are the manifestos about?"

"I can't read much of it because I'm getting nauseated."

"Why? Is it too violent?"

"No. I get car sick if I read on the road. But my first impression is that this guy believes in every conspiracy theory ever conceived."

"Not a guy you want to be stuck next to at dinner."

"And he seems to have the same theory you told me the Friends of Cryptids Society has—that where believers go, so go their supernatural beings."

"Was Arseton one of the guys who got aggressive with me?"

"No. His picture is on here. I'll send you a link to his site."

"Is there any mention of ghouls on there?" I asked.

"I don't think so, but I'm feeling sick to my stomach."

"Okay, stop reading. I think you'll agree that we've found a group of psychos with swords whose mission is to destroy the supernatural."

"Yeah. They're going after witches, like you, and monsters. Presumably, ghouls."

"I think the Osmans were right: someone went to their house with an iron sword to kill ghouls. Ben Nogging showed up with a package at the worst possible time, saw the attacker, and was killed because of it. The attacker then fled without going inside."

"But what about all the people disappearing around town? These psychos with swords wouldn't attack regular people, would they?"

"I think you were right: hungry ghouls were behind those incidents, but they didn't attack the delivery driver. Why would a ghoul prey at another ghoul's house? I believe this Arseton weirdo showed up there to kill the Osmans."

Matt looked at me. "And he and his cronies will try again."

"OUR NEXT STEP is to contact this guy who makes obscure historical weapons."

"Are you going to call him?"

"No." I pulled out the slip of paper the armorer gave me with his information. "I don't want to get a runaround. We're going to pay him a surprise visit."

"*We*?"

"Yeah. You have the day off. And you're too nauseated to do anything else at the moment."

"Will he be open on a Saturday?"

"We'll soon find out."

Just off the main road, between Jellyfish Beach and Sea Lice Sound to its south, was a street that was zoned industrial. There were warehouses, small factories, and long buildings with bays that housed mechanics, electricians, and other contractors and suppliers. Our target, Garth Mulvaney, had his shop in one of these buildings.

"Mulvaney Metalworks," read the sign. "Custom railings, fences, and barbarian weaponry."

"Did I read the sign correctly?" Matt asked. "Barbarian weaponry? This part of town is where you buy stuff for your kitchen renovation, not for fighting the Roman legions."

"So, he's a little quirky."

"Are we over-dressed for buying barbarian weaponry?"

"You are. You should probably go shirtless."

He didn't take my advice. I parked and was relieved to see the shop was open. We went inside. The space was dark and filled with examples of the wares that probably kept him in business: wrought-iron gates, various types of handrails, lots of intricate decorative scrollwork. The guy was talented.

No one was around, so we followed the sound of metallic banging. In a back room was a classic blacksmith's forge, with a blazing furnace and a large man hammering a sword upon an anvil. He wore a leather apron and gloves, plus a face shield.

"Mr. Mulvaney?" I yelled, to be heard above the din of banging.

He looked up. "Are you the woman who ordered the Viking shield?"

"No, we're here to ask you a few questions. I'm Missy and this is Matt. An armorer at the Renaissance Festival gave us your name. Do you make iron swords and axes?"

"I forge swords. I'm kind of backlogged now, though. I'll need a few months to make you one."

"I can't wait," Matt said. "I have villages to sack this weekend."

I elbowed him in the ribs. "Do you sell many iron swords?"

"Not so many," Mulvaney said. "Lots of steel swords, of course. But I'm best known as the only maker of Bronze Age weapons in South Florida."

I guessed I was supposed to be impressed. "Good to know."

"I have thousands of followers on YouTube. Perhaps you've seen my videos?"

"Of course," I lied.

He stuck the sword in a barrel of water with loud hissing, then placed it aside. Unexpectedly, he opened a laptop on a nearby table.

"I'm trying to sell my show to the History Channel," he said, pulling up a video. "It's really unique, because we don't just show the fabrication, but we also use the weapons in historical re-enactments."

"Great," Matt muttered.

"There's a lot of glamor to the late Bronze Age, thanks to *The Iliad* and *The Odyssey*. Here I am as Achilles at Troy."

He played a video of himself strutting on the beach wearing nothing but a loincloth and a bronze helmet, carrying a shield and brandishing a sword. Why was his body all oiled up?

"Back to the topic of iron swords," I said.

"Wait, watch this combat sequence."

Another nearly naked man came into the shot, and the two pretended to sword fight with their short bronze swords. Until they resorted to wrestling on the sand.

"Okay, now about those iron swords," Matt said, stepping around the table so that he couldn't see the laptop screen.

"Have you sold any recently?" I asked.

"No. A couple last year," said Mulvaney, still admiring his own video, oblivious to our embarrassment. At last, he closed the laptop. "Only the most particular collectors insist on iron swords."

"Are any of these collectors in Jellyfish Beach?" Matt asked.

"Funny you ask. I did receive a local order two years ago. I wish I could meet the person so we could talk about weaponry."

"Why can't you meet him or her?"

"He demanded anonymity. I hope you aren't going to ask me who it was."

"Nope," I said. "Why would I do that?"

As we drove away, Matt rubbed his face.

"I'm never going to un-see that video," he said. "I hope I don't get the urge to watch gladiator movies."

"I'm frustrated we got this close, only to hit a dead end. At least, we know that someone in Jellyfish Beach bought an iron sword. But where do we go from here?"

"Maybe there's a club for ancient-sword collectors?"

"The murderer is unlikely to be a member of a club," I said glumly.

"Okay, then where did he find out that iron is deadly to ghouls? That's not common knowledge. I couldn't even find any reference to it on the internet. If we can locate the source of this information, it could lead us to him."

"Sure, no problem. We'll head to the Ghoul Information Center."

"You don't have to be sarcastic." Matt looked out the window and sulked.

"Ghouls know about iron, but they're not going to tell a human. I didn't realize we had ghouls living here full time until I met the Osmans. They keep such a low profile. Acceptance Home Care has no ghoul patients as far as I know."

"Someone must know about ghouls. With all your monster connections, you're my best bet for finding out who it is."

The witch with the most monster connections. Is that going to be my legacy?

NIGHT HAD FALLEN as we drove back into town. Ever since we left the metal shop, Matt's phone had been buzzing with news alerts. That's what you get when you hang around with a reporter.

"Are you going to check your phone already?" I asked.

"I was trying not to be rude." He retrieved his phone from his pocket and scrolled.

He grunted.

"What is it?" I demanded.

"There was a disappearance today. Who knows, maybe a ghoul was involved."

"Why do you say that?"

"Someone was abducted. Wait." He scrolled on his phone. "Oh, no. This is serious. This is bad."

"What? Stop being so opaque."

"Remember Detective Shortle from the Osman house the other night? It's her. She was taken."

CHAPTER 17

CRIME IN MY OWN BACKYARD

Matt said the news updates didn't mention where Detective Shortle had been abducted. I wish they had. It would have prepared me for what I would encounter after dropping Matt off and returning home.

Police cars were parked along my front lawn, four of them. Being that the Jellyfish Beach Police Department was laughably small, this was nearly the entire fleet.

A hefty officer, whose stripes said he was a sergeant, confronted me as soon as I pulled into my driveway.

"Are you the homeowner?" he asked when I got out of my car.

"Um, yes."

"Where were you for the last two hours?" His massive belly blocked me from going anywhere. I'd wisely put the box containing my sword in the trunk.

"At a metal shop on Industrial Avenue. Before that, we were at the Renaissance Festival."

"*We?*"

"I was with my friend, Matt Rosen. He's a reporter with *The Jellyfish Beach Journal.*"

"I know who he is. Little pain in the butt."

"I heard in the news that Detective Shortle was kidnapped," I said. "Are you telling me it happened here?"

The sergeant nodded, and his belly jiggled along with the motion.

"That's her car over there." He pointed to an unmarked sedan parked behind the row of patrol cars.

"Why was she here?"

"Obviously, to speak with you."

"But why? She'd already interviewed me after the murder that happened two houses down."

"You tell *me* why she needed to speak with you."

This guy would never become a detective. I had a feeling he was going to spend the rest of his career doing accident investigations.

Another car pulled up, and a stocky older man in plainclothes got out. He was dressed as if he had come straight from the golf course. I recognized him as Glasbag, the detective who showed up after Shortle at the murder scene. I wondered if he and Shortle were the only detectives on the force.

By now, neighbors were gathering in front of my house, curious about the police activity. This was the kind of thing I wanted to avoid. Old Man Timmons and the Diddlebums were there. Even Fred Furman, who didn't live on this street, had sniffed out the police and the opportunity to gossip.

Glasbag looked sunburned and annoyed. I guess he wasn't used to an actual crime interrupting his post-golfing engagements. He walked right up to me and studied my face. He was at least a foot shorter than I.

"Are you the homeowner?" he asked, studying a slip of paper. "Missy Mindle?"

"Yes."

"I'm Detective Glasbag." He opened a badge wallet and held it toward me.

"Yes. We've met before."

"Did you have an appointment with Detective Shortle this evening?"

"No. I didn't know she was coming here. I was away all day and got home just now. Why did she want to see me?"

"I assumed it was because of the murder on your street. And I saw in the files that a bag of bones was found in your yard."

"Someone must have tossed it there."

He wasn't listening. "Do you have a doorbell camera or any other video security?"

"Yeah. A doorbell camera. Let me see if there's any video."

I unlocked my phone and checked the app for my doorbell camera. I was reluctant to do it in front of the detective because you never know what sorts of creatures could have been in front of my house. Being a witch, I seem to be a magnet for all kinds of freaks, even during the daytime, and it could be embarrassing if the video captured a troll or an enchanted gopher tortoise at my door.

I held the phone so Detective Glasbag could see it, too. The video had kicked in when Shortle parked in front of the house and approached the front door. She was wearing civilian cloth-ing, and I wouldn't have known she was a cop if I hadn't already met her. She rang the doorbell, knocked, and grew impatient, looking into the sidelights next to the door. Then, she peered into the living room window.

I glanced at Detective Glasbag. He seemed embarrassed by Shortle's nosiness.

She disappeared from the frame, probably to peer into other windows.

I was about to exit the video when a UPP delivery truck sped past the camera and down the street.

"These delivery companies must spend so much on gas these days," I said.

Glasbag wasn't listening. In fact, he wasn't standing next to me anymore. He was walking along the front of my house, retracing Shortle's steps. He disappeared around the corner.

What was I supposed to do? Did I have to wait in my driveway, or could I go inside? Should I follow him around as if he were a contractor giving me an estimate? All but one of the cop cars had left by now. The remaining officer stayed inside his car.

Just as Glasbag appeared, coming around the other end of my house, a UPP truck pulled up behind the cop car. Glasbag hurried to the truck, and so did I to eavesdrop.

"A truck like yours was videotaped passing this house two hours ago. Was it you?"

"Yeah," the driver said from the cab. He was the handsome, gray-haired one. "That's why I'm here now. I was driving by and saw the police car, so I knew something might be wrong."

"Please explain yourself," the detective said.

"This is my regular route. When I drove by here earlier, I saw an unfamiliar car parked in front, and the homeowner's car was not here. A woman was walking around, looking in the windows, like she was a burglar."

Glasbag harrumphed. "She's a police detective."

"After she went into the backyard, I saw an elderly woman neighbor I recognized cutting through the yard of the house next door and then going into the backyard of this house. I was suspicious but couldn't stick around because of the tight schedule they have me on. When I drove by just now and saw the cop car, I worried that something bad might have happened to the ladies."

"You say you recognized the elderly neighbor?"

"Yeah. From two houses up the street." He pointed toward the Osmans' home. "Where the driver from my company was murdered."

Could it have been May? I wondered. Her sisters wouldn't have been foolish enough to attack someone in their neighborhood. May, though, had clearly gone feral. It wasn't a stretch to imagine her abducting the detective. I hoped she wasn't planning to eat her.

"Did you see any signs of violence in my backyard?" I asked Glasbag.

He stared at me through squinted eyes. I didn't think he was going to answer, but he surprised me.

"I found her weapon on the ground. Please don't go into your backyard or allow anyone else to do so. We're going to cordon it off with crime-scene tape."

"As long as you can't see the tape from the street. I already have a reputation for being a weirdo, and I don't need it to get worse."

"Just wait until the reporters show up," he said with a smug smile.

Great. Just great, I thought darkly. Then, I looked at the bright side: maybe the crime-scene tape and the news vans would discourage others from snooping around my house.

Namely, my enemies. Today, I learned the Knights Simplar were among them.

Two days later, I learned they were on a true witch hunt.

Monday morning, I showed up at the botanica in a foul mood. You would be in a bad mood, too, if you spent your Saturday night and Sunday trapped at home while reporters banged on your door and did live shots from your front yard. My neighbors were truly entertained by the sight. And I was embarrassed once again.

Luisa and I had yet to begin work on expanding the shop into the former seafood takeout restaurant next door. It seemed some contractors we approached were spooked by the exoticism of the botanica.

"I ain't gonna work for devil worshippers!" more than one of them insisted.

Trying to explain the difference between the devil and the quasi-dark nature of some voodoo gods and Santeria spirits was too subtle for them.

As a result, I couldn't build up our clientele of witches like me. Right now, I didn't mind so much. It meant less work for me when I had too many distractions.

Distractions like the dude who walked in just before

lunchtime. He pretended to browse the shelves of Santeria orisha statuettes, but he didn't look like a Santeria practitioner. I know you can't judge a book by its cover, but this guy was advertising The Book of Dork. I mean, who goes shopping wearing a Renaissance-era outfit of tunic and tights?

That could get you beaten up going out in public outside of the confines of a festival, even in a small town like Jellyfish Beach. We don't have gangs, but I know of several octogenarians who would kick this guy's butt if he crossed their paths.

Wait, I recognized him from his photo on his website. This was Lord Arseton. He wasn't here to buy a good-luck charm or a statuette of Elegua. He was here to judge us.

"Hey," I said as he emerged from an aisle. "I know Mondays are harsh, but the weekend is over. It's not the make-believe Renaissance anymore. It's the real world now."

He looked down at me superciliously. Although he was barely taller than I was, he still managed to look down.

"I know not of what you speak," he said, with a fake English accent.

"Your outfit. In this neighborhood, guys wear shorts or jean, and a T-shirt. Not a Robin Hood costume."

he coming from my yoga class."

construed as yoga pants, but the

Nevertheless, I let it

my sweet shop-

agonists.

store?" he asked,

ptoes to reverse the

power play. "We cater to people's spiritual and health needs. We carry supplies for folk medicine and religious rites. Many of our customers are immigrants from Latin America and the Caribbean who follow the faiths that combine West African religion with Christianity. They live in a hard, unfriendly world and come to us for healing, spiritual support, and a sense of community."

He didn't seem to buy what I said, and looked around, grabbing a porcelain figurine.

"What is this creature?" he demanded.

"That is Chango, a Yoruba god combined with the Catholic saint Santa Barbara. Perhaps you've heard of him?"

"Then what is this?" He held up a different statuette.

"Um, that's Papa Legba."

"Is he a Catholic saint?"

"No. He's a voodoo god."

"Aha! I knew there was something nefarious afoot here."

"Not at all," I said yet again. "Most of our customers attend mainstream churches. But they also practice Santeria, voodoo, obeah, and other faiths that were created after Africans were taken to the New World as slaves and kept the religious traditions of their homelands."

He wasn't listening. He roamed the tight aisles, looking for merchandise to object to.

"And this? What is this? Some form of demonic poison?"

"No. That's a cream for sore muscles. Can I ask what you're looking for here?"

"I lead the Knights Simplar. We are a holy order that seeks to rid the world of creatures that are abominations in the eyes of God. Evil creatures summoned in Satanic rituals or worshipped in depraved barbaric religions."

"Okay. But what's your day job? Just asking."

"I repair smart phones."

"Oh, so if I crack my screen, I can come to you?"

"Don't attempt to distract me. I have a greater mission. The world is besieged by the forces of evil. These forces are allowed into our world by people, deliberately or by accident. This store, and your customers, are inviting evil creatures here. By congregating, by doing your demented rituals, you open the doors to Hell. When you believe you're performing a ritual to heal someone, you're really encouraging a demonic spirit to enter our world."

"I did not know that. I'm sorry our store does not meet your approval. But it's totally legal, and I haven't heard of any priests or pastors denouncing us."

"Then, it is up to me to denounce you."

"Then, I suggest you get out of here and never come back. Here's some molasses candy." I handed him a small bag as I attempted to herd him out of the shop. "It's great for a sore or scratchy throat from screeching at sinners."

Just as I got him near the door, a clattering arose from the back room. It sounded like furniture being knocked over. Luisa had been meeting in there with Madame Tibodet, the voodoo priestess we're partnering with. She will begin providing private consultation sessions for our customers, which will attract more retail business from voodoo practitioners. It had sounded like a good idea.

Until now. When Carl the Zombie came shuffling out of the back room.

I have nothing against zombies when they leave me alone. Contrary to popular culture, they don't roam the earth in packs looking for human brains to consume. Rather, they perform specific duties for their creators and are usually strictly supervised.

I'd grown fond of Carl. Normally, he came here on errands for Madame Tibodet. Today, he accompanied her like a young child who needed supervision.

A bored child, who staggered down an aisle toward the front of the store, accidentally knocking merchandise off the shelves. He was impossible for Arseton not to notice since Carl was clearly a reanimated dead dude in a decaying funeral suit.

Thanks Carl, I thought, for showing up when I had a deluded religious fanatic in the store.

"What is *that?*" Lord Arseton demanded. He looked frightened. It was probably the first time he had actually seen one of the creatures he railed against.

"That's Carl. Pay him no mind. He's just the assistant to a priestess we work with."

Carl moaned. I think he was just saying good morning in a zombie manner, but it didn't come across as friendly.

Lord Arseton squealed.

Carl the Zombie reached the front of the shop and picked up a ceramic figurine of a cat that was sitting on the counter. I don't know if it represented any deity or spiritual entity. I just thought it was cute. And apparently Carl did, too. He turned around, ceramic cat in hand, and returned to the back room.

Where was Lord Arseton?

He stood on the sidewalk just outside of the open door.

"It's interesting that you noted my attire," he said. "Because

I know you were at the Renaissance Festival this past weekend. My fellow knights reported to me that you're a witch."

I was shocked. How did he find out who I was and where I worked? He probably knew where I lived, too.

"Prepare to meet divine justice," he said in a voice like an amateur stage actor. "My holy order will drive you, your zombies, and your other evil abominations from our town and straight to Hell where you all belong."

"Hey, you wouldn't happen to own an iron sword?" I asked.

"I own several swords, and I know how to use them. Beware."

He turned and strode away in his tights and tunic. I wanted to laugh at him, but I felt like a stone had dropped into the pit of my stomach. This guy was going to be a major problem for us.

Laughter erupted from the back room. How would I deal with this new threat? I had to do something before anyone got hurt.

Unless I was already too late.

CHAPTER 18
GHOULS' NIGHT OUT

S ol Felderberg raised his bony hand to volunteer to read first. The members of the vampire creative-writing group leaned forward to better hear, since Sol didn't volunteer often.

"The angst of immortality fills my endless nights," he read from a notebook filled with handwriting. "Four hundred and fifty years I have trod this earth, watching mortals die and buildings razed. Cities grow, and certainty fades. This is the fate I was given when I was turned and raised from death."

"He's so serious," Marjorie whispered. "I was hoping this would be an adventure tale."

I gave her a stern look to shut her up.

"Everything changes, yet all remains the same," Sol intoned in his Boston accent. Completely bald with pointy ears, Sol looked just like the eponymous character in the early vampire movie *Nosferatu*. Except for his Boston Red Sox T-shirt.

"To fit in among the mortals, I must adapt to all the

trends and fashions. Neckties are narrow. They get wider. And wider, still. Then, they get narrower. And narrower still. Before they evolve yet again. Lapels are narrow. Then they get wider. . .”

"Is there no romance in this story?" Gladys asked.

I shushed her.

"And music. I grow to like certain music, and then it's out of style. The younger vampires make fun of me for listening to it. They say, why aren't you liking the latest trendy stars, like Beethoven? Because Beethoven was a punk! But I try to keep an open mind. I listened to him for a couple of hundred years and finally grew to like him. But look what happens—he's not in anymore. Now they have Hip Hop. How long will that last? Why can't I go back to listening to lutes?"

"So, this is more of an essay than a story?" Marjorie asked.

"I think it's free-verse poetry," Gladys said.

"Please hold your comments until Sol is finished," I said.

"Sounds more like whining to me," Doris muttered.

"Time marches steadily onward while I stand frozen," Sol continued. "Alone with my memories of when I was alive. They say you should savor every moment, because soon they will be gone. What they don't tell you is how many other freaking moments you must endure. On and on and on. Immortality is a burden. Do you realize how many times I've had to remodel my kitchens to keep up with the design trends? They're evil, these interior designers."

"Is this part of your essay, or are you just complaining?" Martin asked.

"Nothing is eternal, except a vampire's travails. The end."

Gladys applauded. "I enjoyed the dark tone," she said.

"My son was drinking buddies with Edgar Allan Poe," Sol explained. "I think his work is where I picked up the darkness."

"Missy, you seem preoccupied," Gladys said to me.

"Huh?"

"You're off in another world."

"Sol's essay caused my mind to wander. I have a bunch of problems lately."

"You can share them with us, if you'd like," Marjorie said.

Everyone else agreed. It was obvious they didn't want to talk about Sol's "essay."

"First," I said, "my problems began with ghouls."

Gladys made a look of disgust. "Foul creatures."

"You guys are familiar with them?"

"Yeah, our hunting grounds overlap sometimes," Sol said. "But those savages don't understand the downside of killing your prey. So, they don't do very well in communities like this. They starve or get killed."

"Also, a delivery driver was murdered near my house."

The entire critique group gasped.

"Murdered how?" Sol asked.

"Dismembered. And the skeletal remains of other dismembered victims were found."

"You mean cut to pieces?" Sol asked.

"Yeah. Possibly eaten, too."

The crowd gasped again. These were creatures who fed on the blood of the living—how could they pretend to be so horrified?

"Did one of your neighbors do it?" Marjorie asked.

"Perhaps. The house where it happened is owned by three sweet, elderly sisters who happen to be ghouls."

"Hence, your ghoul problem," Sol said.

"One of them was charged with the murder of the delivery driver. I'm trying to exonerate her."

"Why?" Marjorie asked. "Even if they are supernatural or mythological creatures, they shouldn't go around eating people. All the creatures in this town know the rule: remain secret at all costs."

"Too many people and creatures keep moving to Florida from up in New York and California and from other countries," Doris said. "It's inevitable you're gonna get folks who don't follow the rules."

"They're driving up the real estate prices *and* they're eating people," Marjorie added.

"I truly hope my neighbor is innocent. But she's making it difficult to exonerate her. Now, a police detective has gone missing from my property, and an elderly lady was seen entering my yard while the detective was there. I think it was my neighbor in human form."

The vampires gasped. They knew how dangerous it was for supernatural creatures if the police were involved. On rare occasions, however, it could be dangerous for the police.

Detective Fred Affird was who I had in mind. He'd suspected for years that Squid Tower was full of vampires, and he went out of his way to expose them, even destroy them. It didn't work out so well for him.

Detective Affird was now a vampire himself, living in Squid Tower. He had to retire from the police force to avoid being revealed. He now provided security for the vampire community and played pickleball almost every night.

"I have another problem you guys should know about," I

said. "I stumbled upon a group of religious fanatics who fancy themselves as monster hunters. They somehow identified me as a witch and almost attacked me. And their leader showed up at the botanica where I work, acting as if it was a den of demons. They're clearly dangerous. If they find out vampires exist in Jellyfish Beach, you guys could be at risk. Agnes should be informed of this."

The vampires enthusiastically agreed.

"Maybe Affird should be involved," I added.

"That would be a wise move," a male voice said behind me. I practically jumped out of my shoes.

Fred Affird stood behind me. He wore his signature stern expression and dark sunglasses. Even when he was human, he wore the shades day and night. The most obvious difference in his new existence was he wasn't wearing a sport coat and slacks. Instead, he wore a tennis shirt and shorts. The pale, lanky vampire didn't look good in white.

"Fred has the best vampire hearing I've ever encountered," Sol said. "You can mention his name out on the beach with the surf roaring, and he'll show up wondering who's talking about him."

"The best hearing and the greatest paranoia," Marjorie said.

"What should I be involved in?" Affird asked.

I repeated the summary of my woes.

"I knew Detective Shortle," he said. "I didn't think she'd make it in Jellyfish Beach. A small town with very little crime, but a lot of hidden monsters, can lull a cop into complacency until it's too late. Sure enough, she's been taken by a ghoul."

"Can you help me?"

"With which matter? You've got a bunch of troubles on your hands."

"Tell me about it. My original goal was to exonerate my neighbors."

"You actually want to help ghouls?"

"They're good ghouls. I mean, I think they are."

"I'm not interested in exonerating any ghouls. But I will help search for Detective Shortle. As a former cop, I feel duty-bound to do that. Regarding the religious fanatics, I appreciate the warning. I'll spread the word to all the residents to be careful. If the fanatics show up here, their lifespans will be dramatically shortened."

"Where do the bad ghouls live?" I asked. "I mean, the feral ones who don't shift into human form and live among us?"

Affird laughed bitterly. "Who says the ones who live among us are good ghouls? Anyway, come with me. I'll show you the kind of place that attracts ghouls."

I followed Affird to the parking garage. We got into a vintage muscle car, a gas-guzzler that rumbled like a giant beast when it idled, echoing off the concrete of the garage. I felt uncomfortable riding alone with him because he used to be an enemy of my vampire patients. Now, he was yet another bloodsucker. Who had me trapped in his car.

"Don't worry, you're safe with me," he said with his left hand on the wheel and his right on the stick shift. "I know they say newly turned vampires are impulsive and unpredictable, but I've always had huge amounts of self-control." He looked at me and sniffed. "You're lucky: Type A positive is my least-favorite flavor."

When he saw my shocked expression, he laughed.

"Dark humor is a job requirement for cops."

Engine roaring, we sped across the bridge over the Intracoastal Waterway and continued west until we reached the interstate highway. We traveled north for several miles until a mountain appeared.

No, there aren't any real mountains in Florida. Fittingly, the only ones we have were created with our garbage. The landfills grew at a pace that matched our soaring population of humans, monsters, and any other creatures that left behind trash. We called this landfill Mount Trashmore.

We exited the highway and traveled down a series of dark side roads until the car stopped at a gate in a tall chain-link fence. Affird got out and unlocked the gate.

"Why do you have a key to the county landfill?" I asked when he got back in the car.

"I was an effective cop. I made sure I could go anywhere I needed."

We rolled slowly onto the grounds. During the day, the mountain looming ahead of us would be crawling with bulldozers spreading and flattening the garbage, while teeming flocks of seagulls dive-bombed the scene, looking for rotten food and vermin.

We pulled up near the bays where the garbage trucks dump their contents. Affird made no move to get out of the car, so neither did I.

"I assume the ghouls come here to forage?" I asked.

Affird nodded, his dark shades reflecting rays from the security lights outside.

"As you can imagine, there's a lot of rotting meat here. Also, dead animals, like pets and roadkill."

"Ghouls prefer humans," I said. "Unless they're facing starvation."

He studied me through his dark glasses.

"A sanitation worker told me human bodies sometimes end up here," I added.

Affird nodded. "I was called here several times when murder victims turned up in the waste as it was dumped from a garbage truck. Usually, they'd been tossed in dumpsters in nearby towns and cities. Sometimes, though, murderers bring them directly here and bury them deep in the pile."

"Really? How do they get through the locked gate?"

"They cut through the fence and avoid the security cameras."

"That's a lot of work: bring a body here, cut the fence, and carry the body to the pile."

"Yeah, but if you bury them right, they'll never be found. Or they'll be eaten by the ghouls. I'm not saying the perps know about the ghouls, but they surely know this is the best place to disappear a body."

This place was creepy enough without me hearing about that.

"Have you ever seen ghouls here?" I asked.

"Yes, I have. When they're really hungry, they get desperate and take risks. I knew about them, as did a few other cops, but we couldn't say so officially. Once, I caught a ghoul feeding on a murder victim I'd searched for. I had to write it up as a coyote incident."

"How much do cops know about the supernatural creatures in Jellyfish Beach?"

"I can tell you I knew more than anyone else. I've killed a

couple of werewolves and staked a vampire, because I was determined to drive all the monsters out of our town. Until I became one of them."

"Talk about feeling conflicted," I said.

"One quality I've gained, besides eternal life and heightened capabilities, is a broader perspective. We're all God's creatures, even the monsters. Fear comes from ignorance, and I'm a better soul now that I see the world from a monster's perspective."

Pretty deep words for a vampire cop. I didn't know how to reply.

"We're all God's creatures," he repeated. "Except for ghouls."

A high-pitched chittering sound came from the base of the landfill. I thought it was from rats. Until Affird clicked the power locks on the door.

And the car rocked as a large creature jumped upon the hood.

It was a ghoul in its natural state. It put its face up to the windshield and sniffed through its nose slits, yellow eyes glowing from deep in their sockets. The creature opened a gigantic mouth, revealing rows of needle-like teeth through which saliva oozed.

My heart pounded so hard I was certain the ghoul could hear it.

The ghoul punched the windshield. I couldn't help but scream.

"Don't worry," Affird said. "I've never had one break in before."

Right. If one had, Affird wouldn't be here to say that.

The roof shook as the ghoul crossed over it and tried to break through the other windows. It jumped onto the ground and tried the door handles.

I was freaking out. "Can't we drive out of here?"

"Look, there's another." Affird pointed to a shadow approaching from the landfill. It was a ghoul walking on all fours.

"We're not on safari. Let's get out of here."

The first ghoul saw the other encroaching on his prey. Both screeched, then charged at each other. They fought savagely, right in front of the car. It was like a dogfight but with naked humanoid creatures—which made it a hundred times more frightening.

They bit and clawed and wrestled on the sandy ground. Affird chuckled. He was actually enjoying the show.

"This is horrifying," I said. "Let's go."

"The feral nature of these creatures is fascinating to me. Well, all fun must come to an end."

He unlocked his door and started to get out.

"Oh, my. Wait—are you crazy?"

"This will be quick," he said.

He got out and opened the back door, retrieving an ax from the floor of the car. He walked briskly but calmly toward the battling ghouls.

By the time they noticed him, he was already upon them, swinging the ax with skill and confidence as if he were a base-ball slugger. He hit each one in the chest.

The ghouls went down immediately. But instead of just lying there, they appeared to dissolve in clouds of dark smoke. Soon, there was nothing left of them but piles of ashes.

Affird returned to the car, popped the trunk open, and dropped the ax in it.

"Is that ax head made of iron?" I asked when he slid back into the driver's seat.

"Iron? I wouldn't know. Why?"

I studied him to see if he was playing dumb. It was impossible to tell in his stony face and eyes covered with shades.

"They say that iron is like kryptonite to ghouls."

"They also say the secret to killing ghouls is to do it with one blow. If it takes multiple blows, they're just going to keep trying to eat you. That's what I've heard."

I knew the advice about the single blow, too. But I wanted to know if his ax was iron or steel. Should I be looking for an axman instead of a swordsman?

"Have you killed a lot of ghouls?"

"Not so many. Tonight, you can add two to my tally. And there will be more to come."

"Did you bring me here because you think Detective Shortle is buried here?" I asked.

"I wanted you to see one of the few places where you can dependably find ghouls. They also frequent cemeteries but keep a low profile there, since the locations are more public than this. Regardless of ghouls, if Shortle can't be found soon, this is where I'd look. For her or any other missing person."

Before it came to that, I had my locator spell I wanted to employ to search for her. It was a Hail Mary play, to be sure, but it was better than simply waiting for the police to succeed or fail.

"Detective Affird—wait, am I still supposed to call you detective?"

"You can call me Fred."

That was too weird for me. "I think I'll call you Affird. Can you do another favor for me? It's critical to cast a spell that might find her."

"What do you need?"

"I need you to sneak into the police station and find something in or on Detective Shortle's desk. An object that's dear to her, that she put a lot of attention into."

"I can't do that. I'm not an employee anymore."

"You're a vampire. If anyone could sneak in there, it would be you."

CHAPTER 19
HAMSTER IN HER HEART

I was in bed before midnight. It seemed as if I was finally transitioning away from my nocturnal existence. But then, the doorbell rang.

I threw on a sweatshirt and yoga pants. To be on the safe side, I wore my vampire-repellant amulet around my neck. Sure enough, it was Affird at the door.

"I went to the station," he said. "They're short-staffed nowadays. I didn't even have to sneak in. I just showed up and shot the bull with the night sergeant while I surveilled Shortle's desk at the far end of the room. Sarge kept mentioning how pale I was. Why wasn't I golfing every day? A little mesmerizing turned off the sergeant's brain while I searched Shortle's desk. When I found what I wanted, I brought him back to consciousness and got out of there with him none the wiser."

"Excellent! What did you get?"

He pulled from his pocket a makeup compact and a tiny, framed photo. It was of a hamster.

"A hamster?"

"Her pet," Affird said. "Based on the way she spoke about the rodent, it was very close to her heart."

"No boyfriend or husband photos? Kids?"

"Nope. Just the hamster."

"Thank you, Affird," I said, taking the photo and compact. "I'll cast the spell tomorrow and let you know what I discover."

Far be it from me to judge someone else's personal life. I just wanted an object that would work for my spell. I didn't believe the makeup compact would be very helpful. When I've seen Shortle, she was wearing very little, if any, makeup. Affird was just being sexist in assuming she would have an emotional bond with her makeup paraphernalia.

Affird seemed reluctant to leave, but I wasn't going to stay up all night casting the spell. Besides, it wasn't smart to be alone at night with a man I didn't know well, vampire or not.

I bid him goodnight and returned to bed, where my cats were waiting patiently for me.

THE NEXT MORNING, I called Luisa to tell her I'd be late in coming in. I explained why, and she was perfectly accommodating. It was a far cry from the response I'd gotten in the past when having to cancel or postpone a home-health visit with a crotchety senior, whether they were a vampire, werewolf, ogre, or troll. They all responded to me like, well, monsters.

After tea and a light breakfast, I set to work setting up my magic circle. I was casting the same locator spell I had used with the plumber's shirt, though it took longer than usual for me to gather my inner energies. They must be slightly drained from all the stress I've been under.

Then came drawing energy from the five elements, each represented by a burning candle on the point of the imaginary pentagram within my circle. When I felt the energy at its peak, almost like the water boiling in my kettle, I focused upon the framed photo on the floor in front of me: an overweight orange hamster wearing a miniature birthday hat.

I forced myself away from sad thoughts about a hamster I had when very young, which received a lot of attention from me at first, and then very little. It allegedly escaped, but I suspected my adoptive father had disposed of it. If this little guy had made his way into Shortle's heart, all the better. And that's exactly how I hoped to find Shortle.

Through the power of her love for the rodent.

I grasped the intricate scrollwork of the gilded picture frame. In my state of heightened energies, I could sense Shortle's own psychic energy left here from the many moments she held the frame and stared adoringly at her beloved pet. In the hard, cold world of police work, she found solace in thoughts of her special rodent friend.

I recited the words of the spell, consolidating the energies in my core and pushing them out from inside me. They combined with Shortle's psychic energy and created a glowing orb that floated in the air above the picture frame.

"Go find the soul to which you belong."

The orb rose into the air, magically connected to my mind. As it neared my kitchen ceiling, I saw myself from its perspective: a forty-something in a sweatshirt and yoga pants, kneeling on the floor within a magic circle. Looking up as if I'd been caught doing something embarrassing.

I was breaking a fundamental rule of magic. You must immerse yourself in the fantastic, perform strange rituals, and believe things that to a layman would look silly. But never, ever step back and see yourself from the layman's perspective. Because if what you see appears absurd, your magic will fail.

Note to self: don't do this again.

Fortunately, the orb passed through the wall of my house, and I forgot about myself as I started receiving the images seen by the orb. It was flying above my neighborhood, heading west.

I made note of landmarks as the orb passed them. This was a complicated spell, but even more difficult was the necessity to use non-magical means of locating your target once the orb found it. I identified a major east-west street below as Jellyfish Boulevard. I recognized the Mega-Mart and its giant parking lot off to the left. A system of small lakes below.

We were past the city limits now and above unincorporated suburbia. The landscape became mostly newer subdivisions on land that used to be vegetable farms. The orb angled southward and descended until it was above a community filled with identical houses and streets ending in cul-de-sacs.

Now, things got tricky. I memorized all the visuals I was experiencing so I could compare them to a satellite map when I wasn't focused on the spell. As the orb dropped to about ten feet above the ground, I commanded it to pass close to street signs.

The last sign I saw as the orb slowed was Cormorant Court. And now, as it moved toward a beige stucco one-story home with a barrel-tile roof, I picked up the home number on the mailbox.

Okay, so I lied. This time, the orb made it easy, giving me the exact address.

The orb passed through the home's front door, moved through the foyer, crossed through a kitchen and family room, and entered a hallway with bedrooms. It passed through the open door of the master bedroom and hovered above a large cage where a fat hamster sprawled beneath a running wheel it obviously never used. It was clearly the hamster from the photo.

But where was Detective Shortle? The orb was composed of her psychic energy. It was supposed to find her, not the hamster.

I tried to force the orb away from the pet and toward its target. It rotated, giving me a panoramic view of the room. In the unmade bed was a large lump beneath the comforter.

Is this lump Detective Shortle? Could she be dead? Is that why the orb didn't hover right above her?

This was alarming. Someone must check on her. I called the police department and asked for Detective Glasbag.

"He's not available now. Can I take a message?"

"This is urgent."

"The department is having a team-building outing today. He'll return your call when they get back from the water park."

"Are you serious? They're at a water park? This is about Detective Shortle. I've located her, but she needs immediate medical attention."

"I'll pass along your message. Hopefully, they're not all on the water slides."

I hung up in frustration and called 911 before getting in my car and racing to the house.

When I arrived at Shortle's community, I was expecting to get a hard time from the gate guard, since I wasn't on the guest list. Instead, I found the gate itself had been dismantled and lay on the ground beside the gatehouse. I drove through and, with the help of my mapping app, found Shortle's street.

Oh, my. It appeared my calls got through.

Her street was blocked off by military armored personnel carriers marked with the insignia of the Sheriff's Office. The entire block in front of Shortle's home was filled with law enforcement officers. The Sheriff's SWAT team was here along with dozens of deputies. Jellyfish Beach Police Department officers milled about, some of them still in their bathing suits.

Wasn't this overkill for a woman with a medical emergency?

I spotted Detective Glasbag, strutting around in bathing trunks and T-shirt, barking orders. His legs were awfully skinny for such a stocky guy.

Then, a tight formation of armored SWAT-team members carrying shields and a giant battering ram trotted to the front door and knocked it in with a single blow. A second crew, carrying assault rifles, swept inside.

"She needs medicine, not guns," I said to no one in particular.

More officers went inside. I waited, along with the rest of the army.

Finally, after several minutes, the personnel filed out of the house. Engines fired up. Armored vehicles, vans, SUVs, and squad cars rolled down the street and left the community.

I was the only one left, along with a half-dozen Jellyfish Beach officers in their wet swimwear. Glasbag spotted me and strode over to me, visibly angry.

"You called this in?" he asked.

"I said she had a medical emergency. Not that it was a hostage situation."

"Yeah, the Sheriff tends to overreact. The county gives him such a giant budget, he has all this hardware he needs to find an excuse for. But don't distract me—you could be facing a charge of making a false report."

"Why?"

"Detective Shortle is not here."

"But I saw her?"

"How?"

Oops. I couldn't mention my magic. "I peeked into her window and saw her under the covers."

"There are pillows and a large teddy bear under her covers. She's not here."

Oh, my. I messed up big time. I'd never had a spell fail me like this before. For some reason, it found the hamster instead of the woman who loved it.

"Sorry," I said. "Honest mistake."

Glasbag growled, shaking his head. He walked away muttering, and I slipped away to my car as quickly as I could.

During the drive home, I stewed in my shame. I couldn't figure out what went wrong with the spell. Perhaps, it was that moment when I looked down on myself from the orb's perspective above me. Maybe, it was my lifelong insecurity and excessive self-criticism. I felt absurd—if only for a second—and it messed up the spell.

I've been a practicing witch for years now. I was pretty darn good and getting even better. Why would I let the self-doubt in?

Ladies, you know where I'm coming from, right? We're always too hard on ourselves.

Nevertheless, I still felt obligated to find Shortle. I would try my locator spell again, this time with the makeup compact. I'd been too quick to dismiss its value when Affird gave it to me.

Although my confidence was shaken, I immediately set about casting the spell again. Magic was like riding horses: if you fall off, you need to get right back in the saddle. Before the horse kicks you in the head.

I created my circle, lit the candles, and gathered even greater energy than before. The compact held more psychic energy than I had supposed. I got the sense that Shortle used it frequently, but more for the mirror than for the powder puff. Looking at her reflection made the energy especially focused on herself.

The orb took shape quickly and with plenty of power. When I established a visual connection with it, I avoided looking down upon myself kneeling on the kitchen floor this time. The orb seemed eager to reunite with its soul, like a puppy straining against a leash. I sent it on its way.

After it left my house, it meandered around my neighborhood as if it was getting its bearings. It hovered over the garage of a neighbor across the street. They were snowbirds who spent the warm months in New York. Their house here was empty, and the windows were covered with hurricane shutters.

The orb lost interest in their garage and moved on down the street. Had Shortle been kept in the garage temporarily?

Passing methodically through the streets of the neighborhood as if it were on a tour, the orb kept moving until it reached a more affluent area about two miles from my home. When I say more affluent, I mean the standard homes built in the mid-twentieth century were getting knocked down and replaced by colossal show homes.

The orb arrived at a 1950s concrete-block ranch home that was soon to be destroyed. Many of the windows were boarded up with plywood, and the ceramic tiles of the roof had already been removed. The orb passed through a piece of plywood into the bare interior of the house.

And there was Shortle. She was alive, lying bound and gagged on the dusty floor.

I grabbed a kitchen knife, a first-aid kit, and a tote bag filled with healing herbs and potions. Jumping into my car, I kept myself from exceeding the speed limit and arrived in the neighborhood. I had recognized the general area from the images the orb had sent me. Finding the house was easy. It stood out like a blackened tooth among the brand-new homes that had popped up around it.

The front door was missing its hardware and was fastened with a padlock. I paused to cast a spell to unlock it. I smiled with amusement at an old package-delivery notice that was still stuck to the door.

Detective Shortle was in good condition. She had no

apparent injuries. When I removed her hood and gag, she didn't seem parched from thirst or weak from hunger.

"Who do you want me to call to say you're safe?" I asked.

I expected a husband or relative. Instead, she told me to call Glasbag. Of course, he wasn't available. I told the receptionist that Detective Shortle was safe and where we were.

"How did you find me?" Shortle asked. She thrust her bound wrists toward me, impatient for me to cut the plastic zip tie. I sawed through it with a serrated kitchen knife.

"Oh, a little intuition."

"What do you mean?"

"Do you know who kidnapped you?" I asked, to change the subject.

She shook her head. "It was a man. That's all I know."

"Oh, so it wasn't an elderly lady? You weren't taken down by a sweet seventy-something woman who's been accused of murder?"

"She didn't seem so sweet when she fought her way out of the county jail. How can you be so sure she didn't hire a man to abduct me?"

May didn't appear capable of having a working relationship with a human male, but I couldn't say that.

"Why were you investigating my house?" I asked.

"There's something odd about you. I won't lie. And you seem too friendly with the Osman family."

Time to change the subject again. "So, you were snooping around in my backyard. What happened next?"

"I never heard him or saw him. Suddenly, he tackled me and pulled that nasty hood over my head. He tied my wrists and ankles in seconds and threw me over his shoulder. Then he tossed me in the trunk of a large car or the back of a van. I couldn't tell what kind of vehicle, but it had a loud engine. He took me somewhere nearby and put me in a garage. That night, he came back and moved me to this house."

"Was there anything about him that stood out?"

"No. He didn't talk to me. Even when he brought me a sandwich and water and let me go to the bathroom. The only thing I noticed about him was he was extremely sweaty."

That didn't narrow things down much in a South Florida summer.

"His car or van must have been old, though. It didn't have automatic transmission. He used a stick shift. I could hear the grinding gears."

"Like a muscle car?"

"I'm not sure."

"Do you think he's the serial killer?" I asked.

"Serial killer?"

"Yeah. The killer of the delivery driver. And the one who put the bones on the Osmans' lawn and mine. The person responsible for several disappearances in the last couple of years."

"We didn't want the public to know we suspected a serial killer is here in Jellyfish Beach. You're the first civilian who put it all together."

Actually, I wasn't. I suspected ghouls were responsible for the disappearances but couldn't say that. I was bluffing when I mentioned a serial killer. But now that I knew Shortle was abducted by a man, and the police were investigating a possible serial killer, it made me wonder if a human—not ghouls—was to blame for the disappearances. Or perhaps both species were preying upon our citizens at the same time.

"Why do you think he didn't kill you right away? Because you're a cop?"

"He told me I would have to wait to learn my fate because he was too busy to deal with it right then. But I honestly believe he was shocked when he saw my badge and weapon. I think he assumed I was a realtor or a nosey neighbor snooping around your house."

"That's such a symbol of our current era," I said. "Even serial killers are so busy they're running behind with their murders."

The sound of vehicle doors slamming came from outside. Flashing lights filled the few windows that weren't boarded up.

"Thank you for finding me," Shortle said. "You should know that I won't rest until I figure out how you did it."

CHAPTER 20
NIGHT OF KNIGHTS

Tonight, Luisa and I both left the botanica at 8:00 pm, our usual closing time except on the nights we stayed open later for religious rites or private spiritual consultations. Before I had even driven a block, I realized I was being followed.

It was some sort of dark-colored muscle car. The deep rumbling of its V-8 engine made the car a terrible choice for surreptitiously tailing someone, but I figured they wanted me to know they were behind me. They wanted to intimidate me.

My ancient Toyota, with over 200,000 miles on the odometer, was not capable of eluding them. Therefore, I turned right at the next traffic light, instead of left, and drove toward the police station. Before I reached it, the car's headlights were no longer in my rearview mirror.

I pulled into the parking lot at the police station and considered my options. The street was well-lit here and deserted, giving me a full view of my surroundings.

The muscle car was nowhere to be seen.

I sat there in the parking lot for another five minutes. It seemed silly to phone the police about a car that wasn't following me anymore. And I was eager to get home and feed the cats.

Finally, I lost patience and put my car back into gear. The drive home was without incident, and without dark muscle cars.

The cats were slurping up their canned cuisine, and I was munching on a salad when I heard it.

The engine of a car rumbling on the street outside my house.

I peered through my blinds. The car was parked across the street, one house down in front of the snowbird neighbor who was up north until autumn. The streetlight at the end of the block provided just enough illumination to reveal the silhouettes of two people inside the car.

I called 911 and reported the suspicious car. Next, I quickly created a protection spell. This type of spell comes in a variety of versions and strengths. The most powerful of them forms a protective bubble large enough to surround me, or at the most, my entire house. It can block all but the most powerful magic and keep out creatures that want to eat me. It can even block entry by certain spiritual entities. When the bubble is small and concentrated, even a bullet won't penetrate it.

I had nowhere near enough time to create the super-deluxe version.

Instead, I threw together the discount model, which should be sufficient to keep human thugs from entering the house. It required no elaborate ritual, only the proper energies and magic words.

Protected, I sat by the window and peered through the blinds at the car still sitting there. Headlights swept around the corner, and a police car appeared. It parked behind the muscle car. An officer approached the driver's window and had a brief conversation. The car slowly and smoothly rolled away, disappearing from view.

The police officer crossed the street and came up my front walk.

I quickly dissolved the protection spell before the officer collided with the invisible bubble.

My doorbell rang, and I opened the door. The officer was a pimply faced youth who looked barely old enough to have a driver's license. This must be his first job, at a department that was probably considered the lowest rung of the law-enforcement career ladder.

"Is everything all right, ma'am?" His voice croaked as if he were going through puberty.

"Yes, thanks for checking. I see the car has driven away."

"They sure did. I gave them a stern warning."

I didn't believe this kid was capable of being stern.

"I also ran their license plate, and they have no outstanding violations."

"Thanks for your help."

"Certainly. Call us again if they come back."

I watched the officer walk to his car. It would probably be wise to cast another protection spell. I decided to create a stronger one that would last all night, so I went into the kitchen to use a magic circle this time.

I got down on my hands and knees, drawing a circle around me with the dry-erase marker. Then, I collected the tea candles from a kitchen cabinet, putting them in their places along the circle's circumference. With a grill lighter, I lit the first candle.

And the back door to the kitchen burst open.

Two men wearing ski masks pushed into the room. Even without seeing their faces, I recognized them as the two Knights Simplar from the Renaissance Festival. It was the stooped posture of the taller one, and the heavily tattooed hands of the stout one, that gave them away.

I ran from the room almost as fast as the cats did, following them into my bedroom.

Which wasn't the smartest move, I realized. While Bubba and Brenda might feel safe hiding under the bed, that wouldn't work for me. I was trapped in there, with only my windows as an escape route. Which the bad guys would figure out.

To make matters worse, my phone was still sitting on the kitchen counter. I didn't have a landline anymore. There was no way for me to call the police.

Hearing their footsteps on the hardwood floor of my hall, I quickly threw together the simplest protection spell I had. I wasn't sure how durable it would be, but it would at least buy me some time.

Remembering the day at the festival, my eyes roved to the box sitting in my open closet. My new sword. I didn't have any firearms, but I did have this nice piece of steel.

And it was about time to break it in. I tore open the box.

Adult bodies thudded against a solid surface, but it wasn't my bedroom door. They were trying to get through my rudimentary protection bubble.

"You will not stop us, evil witch!"

With this spell, intruders couldn't get in from the outside. But I could exit from the inside. It was time to throw them off with a surprise attack.

Gripping the sword's handle in my right hand, I unlocked the bedroom door with my left.

I yanked open the door, giving a shrill banshee shriek—my closest approximation of a battle cry.

The two thugs were surprised to see me coming at them. They were at the edge of the invisible bubble, where the hallway met the living room. They were doubly shocked to see the sword.

I ran at top speed, easily exiting the bubble, and plunged the sword into the stomach of the stout guy.

Only, it didn't go into his stomach. This was a bad time to realize the point had not been sharpened. Remember, this was a collectible, not a weapon. It merely poked into his belly fat. He knocked the blade away with his arm.

His sweatshirt's arm was cut, though. The edges of the blade were sharper than I expected. The only problem was, I didn't have room to swing the sword in the narrow hallway.

No, it wasn't the only problem. There was another, more serious one.

Both men pulled pistols from their waistbands.

A broadsword vs. nine-millimeter handguns is not a fair fight.

I retreated to the bedroom and slammed the door just as a gunshot went off. A hole appeared in the door. I jumped to the side.

The protection spell would have to get much stronger right away.

I focused my energies and mouthed the words to the spell.

Another gunshot splintered the doorjamb.

Even if my spell was strong enough to keep the men from getting to me, there was no time to fortify it to stop their bullets. They could shoot the place to pieces and most likely take me and the cats out along with the drywall.

As if one of the men had read my thoughts, a bullet flew into the room at a different angle, piercing a wall of the closet. And one of my dresses.

Why couldn't it have ripped through my old scrubs instead?

I took cover on the floor. From my new perspective, I could see poor Bubba and Brenda cowering with the dust bunnies beneath the bed.

A loud sneeze came from outside of my bedroom. And I got an idea.

I reached under the bed and grabbed a ball of shed cat hair. Dozens of such gray balls appear in my house daily. But one was all I needed to craft a new spell.

The protein in cat hair and skin that so many people are allergic to is called *Fel d 1*. Perhaps, the thug who just sneezed in my hallway was allergic to cats. Even if he wasn't, enough of the allergen could make anyone have a reaction.

The right magic could make it a very bad reaction indeed.

I didn't know any allergy spells, but I knew a good one for stink bombs. All it required was a particle of a noxious substance. The spell broke it down to the atomic level, reproduced it, and sent it into the air at a high density.

I drew an imaginary circle on my bedroom floor and knelt within it, cupping the cat hair in my hands. Bubba and Brenda were acutely interested in what I was doing with their discarded fur, though they were still too scared to come out from under the bed.

I chanted the words I remembered from the spell, improvising to create this unique version of it.

Avolare! I commanded.

I didn't have to wait long before the sneezing began. Sneezes rattled off like machine guns. The men were convulsing with their *ah-choos.*

A man hit the hardwood floor with a thud. Furniture was knocked over.

Panicked wheezing and whining.

"I'm breaking out—*ah-choo!*—in hives!"

"I can't breathe!"

More furniture crashed to the floor.

Guys, use your brains. Get your butts out of here.

No, they had to knock over more furniture as they convulsed with sneezing and thrashed in near-anaphylactic shock.

I shuddered to think of how many surfaces the germs from their sneezes landed on.

Finally, heavy steps thudded across the living room and kitchen floors. The house fell silent.

I waited for a few minutes before I ventured out of my room, carrying my unhelpful sword. There was no sign of them anywhere as I crept through the living and dining rooms into the kitchen.

The broken door hung at an odd angle. I grabbed my phone

from the island and called 911. A diminishing roar from what sounded like a muscle car came through the open door, but I wasn't about to let my guard down.

I sneezed myself before I remembered to break my spell.

How COULD I get in touch with the Friends of Cryptids Society? They hadn't given me business cards or any sort of contact info. There was no website, of course. They simply showed up at my door when they wanted me.

I had to warn them about the Knights Simplar. The misfits, whom I'd thought were merely a bunch of creepy weirdos, were in fact a serious threat to the supernatural community.

I went into my bedroom closet and unlocked the metal filing cabinet where I keep important paperwork, pulling out my contract with the Society. There, on the last page, I found a telephone number. I dialed it.

"Please leave a message," said the recorded voice that sounded like Mrs. Lupis.

"Hi, this is Missy Mindle. Please contact me ASAP. We're under attack by hostile fanatics that are a threat to the Society's interests."

Yes, my message was vague, but I didn't feel comfortable being more specific in voicemail.

Who knew when they'd get back to me? In the meantime, I had a lot of work to do. My back door needed to be fixed immediately. I spent the better part of an hour putting up a moderately secure protection spell and even threw some wards into the backyard to repel evil spirits.

I lacked the carpentry skills to replace the door, and I couldn't wait for days or weeks for a contractor. No, I didn't have a handyman. Until recently, I was a home-health nurse with no disposable income.

I did, however, know a handy werewolf who owed me a favor. After a quick phone call, Harry Roarke promised to stop by later with a new door from the local home-improvement store. Helping him get out of trouble after he was accused of murdering (i.e., devouring) a human not long ago had put me on his BFF list.

Only a half hour later, the doorbell rang. I hoped Harry would be as handy as he was prompt.

When I answered the door, I found Mrs. Lupis and Mr. Lopez standing on my front porch in their usual gray suits and ties. Mrs. Lupis held a large plastic pet carrier. I couldn't see what was inside.

"We had hoped you wouldn't run into the Knights Simplar this soon, but we were surely naïve," she said.

"We thought a humble botanica would escape their notice," Mr. Lopez added.

"To be honest, I caught their attention at the Renaissance Festival," I said. "I thought all I'd find there would be innocent eccentrics. Not psychopaths."

"Hm, they must have sensed your magic," Mrs. Lupis said.

"Yeah. I've never had that happen before when going out in public, unless it was a fellow witch or wizard."

"I'm afraid to say, from now on, you must be on a war footing. We've brought along someone to help you stay in touch with us. And to help you with your magic by being your witch's familiar."

Uh-oh. I looked down at the pet carrier. "What did you bring? I have two cats already. They won't take kindly to another."

"No worries," Mrs. Lupis said. "We brought you an iguana, a special breed raised in Central America to be familiars for magicians. These lizards are born with the magic gene."

"An iguana? I don't want an iguana."

"Oh, yes you do," Mr. Lopez said. "He'll take your magic to another level."

"I've got to admit, I don't like reptiles. Except for dragons, but they don't make good house pets."

Mrs. Lupis shushed me. "Please don't offend him."

"And I already have a familiar of sorts. A ghost who's tied to a rare grimoire I own."

"A ghost can't be a true familiar," Mr. Lopez said. "A familiar should be alive. Please accept him. Really, we *insist*."

The "insist" was the most adamant word I'd heard so far from the duo.

"Tony worked with a highly accomplished mage, so he really knows his stuff," Mrs. Lupis said. "Unfortunately, the mage needed to re-home him."

"The iguana's name is Tony?"

"You talkin' to me?" said a guttural voice with a New York accent coming from the pet carrier.

"Tony, show her your sweet and charming side if you want to be adopted."

"I don't think I need an iguana from Central America via New York," I said.

"We *insist*," Lopez and Lupis said in unison and with the hint of a threat.

Mr. Lopez pushed past me into the house. I got a glimpse of a large green lizard about four feet long from head to tail.

"Your protection spell is fading fast," Tony said. "You oughta fix that."

"See, he really does know magic well," Mrs. Lupis said. "And as any good familiar, he is telepathic. It will make your working relationship with him even stronger, and he'll be able to reach us immediately if you need us."

"Is he like your spy or something?" I asked.

"Of course not," Mrs. Lupis said. She placed the carrier on my kitchen island. The last place I wanted the iguana was in my kitchen.

Mr. Lopez pointed toward the broken door. "Looks like the Knights Simplar are brutish louts."

"That's what I wanted to talk to you guys about. The impression I get is that they are hunting the very creatures your society wishes to protect."

"We have heard of these simpletons," Mrs. Lupis said. "To the best of our knowledge, they haven't found any cryptids yet."

"Well, they found me," I said. "I'm not a cryptid, just a human witch. But I was instantly placed on their enemy list."

"Did they come here to scare you or to kill you?" Mr. Lopez asked.

"I don't believe they planned this very well. They obviously wanted to scare me, but I had the gut feeling things were escalating, and I would have ended up dead if my magic hadn't worked to scare them away."

My grim words left everyone in silence.

"Yo, is anybody gonna let me out of here?" said the voice in the pet carrier. "I gotta go. Traveling is always murder on my bladder."

"Oh, my," I said, sighing. "Do you need to be let outside?"

"What, you think I'm some kinda animal? I'll have you know I'm litterbox trained. I smell one in this house. Along with two cats."

"Okay, hang on."

I picked up the surprisingly heavy pet carrier and brought it to the laundry room, which doubles as my cats' bathroom. I set the carrier on the floor near the litter box and opened its door.

"Have at it, big guy," I said, leaving the room to give him some privacy.

When I returned to the kitchen, Mrs. Lupis and Mr. Lopez were gone. A note lay atop the island.

Be vigilant, it said.

Thanks for nothing, I thought.

Then, a cat yowled, and I rushed to the laundry room.

CHAPTER 21
WITCH'S FAMILIAR

T arrived in the laundry room to find Bubba atop the washing machine, growling and hissing at Tony. The iguana's head crest was erect, but otherwise, he appeared calm. Bubba, not so much. His tail was puffed out and twitching and his hackles were raised.

"Tell your cat I was just doing my business. Nothing for him to get all territorial over. Though, I might suggest you get a second litter box just for me. I hate cat pee, and I'm sure they're not delighted by mine."

I did not need all this aggravation now. Was it too soon to re-home Tony again?

The lizard strutted from the laundry room, surrendering the litter box to Bubba, who was not sure if he was happy about winning it back.

Tony wandered into the living room.

"Nice place you got," he said, surveying the room. "A little dated, but maybe you're going for the historic, shabby-chic thing."

"In Florida, a house this old is considered historic," I said, a bit too defensively.

"I see. In case you didn't realize, while your cat was doing his macho male displaying act, someone knocked on your front door."

"Really?" I walked to the door and opened it a crack. No one was there. Finally, I noticed the yellow sticky note on the door frame.

"For Pete's sake, I missed a delivery that needed an adult signature. It's Holy Vodka from the Vatican. I need it for a spell I'm creating. Let's see, it says they'll make one more delivery attempt tomorrow. What a pain in the butt."

Tony shrugged. At least, I think it was a shrug. It was more of a reptilian crouching motion.

"How blessed am I! Antonio! What brings you to our humble domicile?"

It was Don Mateo. He had materialized in the fireplace, awkwardly crawling out of it as if he were constrained by the body he mimicked but didn't truly possess.

"You know him?" I asked the ghost.

"Oh, yes, we traveled in the same supernatural circles back in sixteen-oh-two. Antonio was a familiar back then, as well, though he inhabited the body of a Cavalier King Charles Spaniel. How did you end up as an iguana, my old friend?"

"I was reborn at a ranch that raises paranormal lizards. That was like about a century ago."

"Iguanas keep growing as they get older," I said. "If you're that old, you should be as big as my house."

"You know when adults told you not to smoke because it stunts your growth? Well, I didn't listen."

"An iguana that smokes?"

"Those were different times when I picked up the habit."

"What brings you to our home?" Don Mateo asked.

I hadn't realized the ghost considered my home his, too, but it was endearing.

"I was working a gig in New York as the familiar to a mage. He was such a freaking doofus. I don't know how he reached mage status. He blamed all his magic mishaps on me. After he accidentally turned his own legs into insect legs, he dumped me. The Friends of Cryptids Society of the Americas brought me here to Miss Mindle. I hope she doesn't blame her mishaps on me."

He looked at me with sad eyes.

"Madame does not have mishaps," Don Mateo said.

That was kind of him. He obviously didn't know about when I located Shortle's hamster instead of Shortle.

"I won't blame anything on you. I've never had a familiar who was alive, though. What are you supposed to do, exactly?"

"I help you channel your magical energies, cast spells, communicate with the spirit world. I'm like an assistant."

I didn't think I needed an assistant.

"Yeah, you do need an assistant," he said. "Believe me."

I most definitely didn't need a telepathic assistant.

"The telepathy makes me better at my job. I anticipate your needs before you even realize you got 'em. As we were speaking, your ears picked up the sound of a delivery truck driving up your street—the rumbling engine and the grinding gears. You didn't think about it, but the sounds reminded you

210

of what the detective said she heard when she was kidnapped."

"Wow. That's right."

Was Shortle put in a UPP truck when she was abducted? Also, she mentioned her captor was sweaty—as are so many UPP drivers in their cabs without air conditioning.

"Your subconsciousness knows that fact is important. And just now, the sticky note you got from UPP triggered the memory that you borrowed a note from your neighbors. You never used your magic to investigate it. Your subconscious knows this, but your conscious brain is too distracted right now to realize it. Matters like this are where I come in handy."

"Oh." I had completely forgotten about the delivery notice Alex Osman had given me. Or what, exactly, I had intended to do with it.

"You thought it could help Don Mateo connect with the spirit of the murdered driver, but he said the note was left by someone who's alive."

"That's right. It was left by a different delivery driver." The little cogs in my brain turned. "I wonder if it's the same driver who left *my* note."

In other words, the regular driver of the route that includes this street. Does it matter if he left the sticky notes?

"Yes, it matters," Tony said. "Remember the grinding of the gears. Maybe, you'll come across a clue from the delivery notice. Maybe not. But it ain't gonna hurt to look into it."

My mind ran through my inventory of spells. I kept glancing at Tony, expecting the telepathic lizard to hijack my memory and tell me what I was looking for.

"There's a spell in my grimoire," Don Mateo said.

"Oh, I didn't realize you were still here." That's the problem with ghosts—they tend to be invisible and ghostly.

"The spell is among those in the addenda," the ghost said.

My late father, who died soon after I was born, was an accomplished witch. He bequeathed to me a well-known grimoire called *The Key of Solomon*. What made this one unique were the spells handwritten in the empty pages at the back of the book over 400 years ago by Don Mateo when he was a practicing wizard in Florida after fleeing the Spanish Inquisition. This was before his life was ended when he accidentally summoned a demon that wasn't happy to be summoned.

"You'll find the spell in the alchemy section. It provides information about the essences and spirits of substances, both organic and inorganic."

"Okay," I said. "I'll give it a shot."

I RETRIEVED the ancient tome from the locked cabinet in my closet. The book was in surprisingly good condition for its age, its pages appearing to be more like parchment than paper. Flipping to the back of the book, I scanned Don Mateo's intricate inked text, written in archaic Spanish. I was familiar enough with it by now to decipher it, with the help of an old Spanish dictionary and, sometimes, the ghost himself.

I don't know what rituals Don Mateo used to cast spells when he was alive, but I used my usual method within a magic circle, placing the grimoire propped open on a recipe bookstand. After the requisite gathering of my energies and enhancing them with the power of the five elements, I followed Don Mateo's directions carefully.

Each delivery notice was torn into thirds. One piece of each went into my bra to hold it against my heart. And no, the detail with the bra was not written in the directions. The second piece of each was to be chewed and swallowed, which I did with much distaste. The remaining thirds of the notes I placed in a small ashtray and lit on fire using the candle placed on the point of the pentagram representing fire.

Now, I intoned the words of the spell, a mixture of Latin and Hebrew, and waited for something to happen.

Data flowed into my brain. I saw the manufacturing process of the pulp being turned into paper. I saw the printing, cutting, and application of adhesive. The creation of the notepads came next.

I was thoroughly bored. This wasn't helping me at all.

Then, I picked up tiny fragments of psychic energy from various humans who had handled the pad. The amount of energy grew and dominated my consciousness.

Images entered my mind of a delivery driver writing on the notes and checking boxes before sticking them to front doors.

I saw the Osmans' door. I saw mine. A sweaty hand placing the notes.

Then, I received a vision of the driver himself. It was the handsome, older guy I'd talked to before. Random, mundane details came into my head about schedules and manifests.

Darker thoughts flooded into me, as well. Feelings of anger, resentment, fear. Death.

I also received data—traces of many substances the driver's

hands had touched and left upon the notes. There were so many of them, and they meant nothing to me.

Until I sensed traces of blood. It wasn't enough to be visible on the notes or on his hands. It was random blood cells embedded in the whorls of his fingerprints.

And iron. Not the iron found in blood, but from the metal itself. Just a trace of it. But enough to raise concerns.

When the paper had exhausted all the information it could give me, I wiped away a section of the magic circle and ended the spell. I took the remaining third sections of the notes and walked directly to the Osman house.

"WOULD you like some cucumber sandwiches with your tea?" Alex asked as she poured my cup from the teapot. With her close proximity, the light reflecting from her platinum blonde hair nearly blinded me.

"Please don't go to such trouble for me, barging in on you like this."

June was in the kitchen. I sniffed. It smelled distinctly like steaks were in the broiler.

"If I didn't know you guys were vegans, I would swear you're cooking steaks in there."

"They're Unlikely Steaks," June said, appearing in the opening to the kitchen. "You know, the plant-based meat."

"I've heard of Unlikely Burgers," I said. "I didn't realize they made steaks, too."

"They're quite delicious," June said. "We'd invite you to

dinner, but we're told we always woefully undercook our fake meat."

"Thank you, but I'll leave in a moment. Since you sisters are so sensitive to iron, I was wondering if you could detect it on a piece of paper that was handled by someone who touched iron."

"I already detected something the moment you walked into the house," Alex said.

I handed her the pieces of the delivery notices. She reached for them, then yanked her hand away.

"Yes, iron," she said. "Trace amounts, but definitely there."

"You didn't sense it on the notice when you gave it to me?"

"I did, but I was still traumatized by the murder. I thought I was remembering the iron we'd sensed in our yard."

"Can you tell what kind of iron object it was?"

"No, I can't. But almost all the metal people handle nowadays is steel, aluminum, or other kinds. Unless you're cooking with a cast-iron skillet or using a dumbbell."

"Or wielding an iron sword," I said.

"Oh. Now I know why you're asking."

"Yes. I'm wondering if our delivery driver owns an iron sword. I might call upon your iron-detection abilities sometime in the future."

"Don't hesitate to ask."

Finally, I brought up the uncomfortable topic that had been left unmentioned.

"Have you heard from May?"

A breath caught in Alex's throat. "No. No, we haven't."

She was lying; I was sure of it.

"I hope she's okay," I said. "Do you know if she is?"

"I believe she's well. I don't know where she might be, though."

"Of course. Please give her my best if you speak to her. Tell her I promise to find the true killer."

Alex smiled nervously and nodded.

The powerful scent of browning beef and fat drifted from the kitchen. Plant-based, my butt.

CHAPTER 22
DANGEROUS ROUTES

Both Matt and I hit brick walls when we called UPP and asked which driver or drivers had routes that included my street. They claimed they couldn't divulge such information.

"I don't care what their corporate lawyers say. It's not top-secret information," Matt said. "We need an alternative approach."

"Like what? I don't have a spell to hack their computer system."

"I was thinking something simpler. Namely, booze and bribery."

"Really?"

"One of their drivers is a regular at the Ripped Tide. We get on pretty well, and I've used him as a source for stories before. If he agrees to help, I'll tell you to meet us there."

The Ripped Tide was a downtown dive bar, popular with workers at the newspaper, surfers, bikers, and the sorts of folks you don't want to meet in a dark alley. Matt loved the place. I was always afraid of getting an infection there.

Three nights later, Matt called me.

"Bobby came through," he said. "Meet us at the Tide at eight tonight."

The place wasn't too crowded, probably because most of the regulars were in jail. Matt sat at a table near the bar with a young African-American man with dreadlocks and a UPP uniform.

"Bobby, this is Missy."

He stood and took my hand. *"Enchantée."*

"I'll get you a beer from the bar," Matt said. "Brenda, the waitress, is out. She shot her boyfriend again." He returned with a bottle with the cap already popped off, and I thoroughly wiped the opening with a tissue.

"Thank you for helping us," I said to Bobby.

"No problem. I went into the system at our warehouse and printed a couple of old manifests. The computer determines the routes based on the locations of the deliveries. Drivers don't get an identical route every day like mail carriers, but the system assigns us to the same parts of town, based on the assumption that if we know the area, we'll navigate it more quickly."

He spread printed lists on the table.

"All those deliveries are for one driver in one day."

"Wow," I said. "That's insanely busy."

"Right. Of course, all these deliveries will be loaded on our handheld scanners. I searched for your address, and the driver who most often was assigned to it was Alfred Germani."

"Do you know him?" I asked.

218

"Just from seeing him in the warehouse. Older guy. Really intense."

"Is he cute with graying hair?"

"Short, graying hair. I don't know about cute. He was questioned by the police not too long ago."

"Really? Why?"

"He got into a big argument with another driver about a truck. The driver turned up dead later that same night."

"Oh, my. Was he found dead while delivering on his route?"

"Yep. It was the same route Germani usually runs."

"I can't believe the police talked to our guy and didn't tell me," I said to Matt.

"Of course they didn't tell you. They don't believe they need our help in this case. After Bobby mentioned to me about the questioning, I asked him to print some of Germani's manifests."

"Randomly?"

"No. Remember when I came up with the various disappearances in this area over the last couple of years? These manifests are for each date someone went missing."

"Impressive. Germani was working on each of those dates?"

"Almost every single one," Bobby said.

"Now," Matt said to me, "you and I have the fun task of seeing if Germani's routes overlapped with the locations where the missing people were last seen."

"Oh, my. Sounds time-consuming."

"Yes. It's going to be tedious. It would be a rare coincidence if someone disappeared from the same address where a package was delivered, but we can learn if Germani was nearby."

"Tedious, to say the least."

WE THANKED BOBBY PROFUSELY, and I made a donation in his name to his favorite pet-rescue charity. The following day, I worked shortened hours at the botanica, and Matt met me at my house with Chinese food to review the manifests.

"Who is this schmuck you brought home?" asked Tony from the open door to the garage. His sleeping quarters were out there to reduce the number of altercations with my cats.

"Who said that?" Matt asked. "Is there a mobster from New York in your garage?"

"Not quite. It's Tony. He's a supernatural iguana who's supposed to be my witch's familiar."

"I thought cats were familiars."

"Any kind of creature will do. As long as they're magical."

"Does he eat your flower gardens?"

"I heard that, you wiseacre."

Tiny footsteps and the slithering of a dragged tail sounded from the laundry room as Tony came into view.

"Tony, put that cigarette out," I ordered. "I told you there's no smoking in the house."

He stubbed it out on the tile floor, then flicked the butt into the garage with his tail.

"Yeah, he's an iguana all right," Matt said. "With an unhealthy habit. I've never imagined one could talk. I thought you'd just have a telepathic connection with him or something."

"We've got that, but he can also talk. He was born with vocal cords and everything."

"Can he help us cross-reference these manifests?"

"I don't do desk jobs, big guy," Tony said. "I leave that to pencil necks like yourself."

"Do I have to take this abuse from an overgrown gecko?"

"Yes," I replied. "Get used to it."

"Yeah, and you better behave yourself with my witch, buddy."

With that, Tony turned around and strolled back into the garage.

Matt stared at me impassively, then broke out laughing.

"The carnival of weird never ends with you, does it?"

"No," I said. "And something tells me it's just going to get weirder. Now, let's eat and get to work."

To make things easier, I connected my laptop to the TV and filled it with a map of Jellyfish Beach. I pinned all the locations where people had gone missing.

Then came the tedious part. Matt and I each took manifests and read every address, glancing up at the TV screen when we recognized street names, to see if they were near the pins. Most of the addresses we had to look up on our phones and calculate the routes between them, before cross-referencing them with the larger map.

It took hours, all the Chinese food, and several beers. But soon, we had connections between nearly half the disappearances and Germani's routes.

"We've found enough to show a reason to suspect Germani," I said. "The police can finish connecting the dots."

"It's bad enough to be a serial killer," Matt said, shaking his head. "But to use your work vehicle to transport bodies is a real no-no."

It finally dawned on me that a good number of the "disappearances" were murders, unless, as in Shortle's case, the victims were being held alive somewhere. I mean, I guess I knew it deep down inside. "Disappearance" sounds vague and imbued with a sense of hope that the missing would be found. But it could also mean "dead, but the body hasn't been found."

Or, "dead, and the body was buried." Or, in the case of ghouls, it was dinner.

Was Germani a ghoul? The thought of a ghoul coming to people's front doors every day was frightening. And was he the individual who was framing the Osmans? It made sense. He had opportunities galore. He was frequently in the neighborhood, and he had a truck to carry remains to be planted in the sisters' yard.

And dropped in front of my house.

I did a quick internet search. "There's nothing on Germani except for a few social media photos. We need to find out more if we're going to get the police to take us seriously. First, we need to find where he lives."

"We don't need magic to do that," Matt said. "Unless he's staying as a guest in someone's house, we should be able to find his residence, even if he's a renter."

I typed away on my laptop. "There's a record for him on the county property appraiser's site." I looked up the address on a map. "Holy guacamole!"

"What?"

"He lives right next to the landfill. There are ghouls hanging around the landfill, looking for the occasional bodies buried there."

"Bodies he may have put there himself."

"Causing the ghouls to hang around. Maybe even threatening his home. A good reason to own an iron sword, wouldn't you say?"

"Just out of curiosity, how much is his house worth?" Matt asked. "I can't think of a worse location for a home."

I told him what the records showed was the home's value. I did another search and was shocked to see the home was for sale, at double the appraised value.

"This market is simply nuts," Matt said.

"Too many people moving here."

"And too many non-humans, as well."

"Hopefully, our friend Alfred Germani will move to the state prison soon, whether or not he sells his house."

I excused myself to make a phone call.

ALFRED GERMANI'S neighborhood was nicer than I had imagined, or so it appeared in the moonlight. The street was in a rural area with houses on huge lots. Each house was surrounded by enough land to grow vegetables or have small farm animals.

It had probably been a nice, quiet place to live before bad luck and county commissioners conspired to put a landfill next door. You would have thought the stink of decaying organic matter would have forced everyone to sell cheap and move away. The houses we passed all seemed to be occupied, however, with lights glowing inside and out.

I drove us down a straight dirt road that ended at a chain-link fence surrounding the landfill. The fence bordered Germani's backyard.

His home was a modest one-story structure in white stucco with a metal roof and a mailbox shaped like a cow. It looked perfectly normal, if you could ignore the mountain of grass-covered garbage that rose about a hundred yards behind it.

I turned off my headlights and rolled past his driveway. In the house, about twenty yards from the road, the blue flickering light of a television shined through a front window. I turned around and coasted back up the road, stopping by a stand of trees out of view of any homes.

"Okay, that is his house, and we've established someone lives there," Matt said. "Mission accomplished."

I chuckled. "Sorry. We're not done yet."

"Seriously, what do you hope to accomplish? It's not like he's going to invite us in for a beer and volunteer a full confession. Unless you have a miraculous magic spell that can make him do it."

"I have my truth-telling spell, but it won't force him to let us inside."

"Then what are you—I mean, we—going to do?"

"Create a diversion."

CHAPTER 23
TRUTH SPELL

Matt and I crouched behind a thick cluster of saw palmettos that hid us from the house and from the street. We were in a shadowy area on the side of the house, facing the rear. The backyard was dark, but I saw floodlights lining the back wall of the house, probably motion triggered. The chain-link fence bordering the landfill ran the entire length of the yard.

In the silver light of the moon, the fence showed signs of having been cut through and repaired with metal wire. The yard looked unremarkable, but I sensed it was a killing field.

"You won't tell me what the diversion is?" Matt asked.

"You'll find out soon enough."

We crouched in silence. Except for the buzzing of insects in my ears. Whatever, it's Florida. Matt slapped a mosquito on the back of his neck. I shushed him.

Something moved on the landfill side of the fence. Had I imagined it?

No, something was definitely there, approaching the fence. A tall, naked figure.

A pair of glowing yellow eyes.

The floodlights on the rear of the house popped on, filling the backyard with bright light, and revealing the ghoul on the other side of the fence.

A familiar-looking ghoul. It was May Osman, fulfilling my request, relayed through her sisters, to attack the house.

She made quick work of the chain-link fence, ripping the interlocked metal wire as easily as if it were a spider web. It was obvious that this part of the fence had been breached many times before by ghouls scavenging at the landfill and becoming bold enough to go after the nearest living human.

And that particular human knew the drill. A back door burst open, and Alfred Germani, wearing nothing but shorts, flew out into the yard.

I have to admit, he looked good without a shirt.

He carried a massive broadsword. I was pretty sure it was made of iron.

I wasn't about to let him destroy May. Now that we got him out in the open, I could cast the powerful immobilizing spell I had prepared. His limbs seized up, and he fell on his face upon the lawn.

"Okay," I said to Matt. "Let's go."

We ran from the palmettos over to Germani.

"Hi, Alfred," I said. "I'm on your delivery route. Do you remember me?"

I positioned myself so he, with his face on its side in the grass, could see me.

"Yeah."

"You and I are going to have a little talk."

The snapping of metal wires made me look up. May was still coming at us. In her natural ghoul form, discretion was not an option. She was hungry, and the three of us were potential meals.

I grabbed Germani's sword and pointed it at May.

"No, May. Go back to your hiding place. Thanks for your help, but you can't eat us."

She growled and looked ready to lunge.

I stepped toward her, waving the sword aggressively.

May looked at the weapon and recoiled. She made a high-pitched keening sound. I took another step toward her.

She hissed at me, but finally retreated, stepping through the hole in the fence but stopping just beyond the reach of the floodlights. There she stayed, watching us.

I handed the sword to Matt. "Keep an eye on her while I cast my next spell."

"This sword is heavy. But I can handle it. I'm no pencil neck like your iguana said."

"You're a strong man."

May hissed at him.

He let out a shriek.

"A brave man, too."

"Jeez, I hate ghouls," he said. "She looks like one of our state senators."

May finally disappeared into the darkness.

My truth-telling spell was one I learned early in my witch career. It was simple, invented by kitchen witches, and had been passed down for centuries. It required less power than my immobilization spell did but needed special ingredients.

I sprinkled the powder on Germani, especially on his head. I won't tell you what the ingredients are, though you probably have a couple of them in your kitchen spice rack. Other substances required expeditions to the Everglades. And one ingredient I ordered from the internet, and Germani was probably the one who delivered it to me.

Everyone, except the most antisocial, enjoys sharing information. Most people, except pathological liars, prefer to tell the truth. This spell simply inflames those urges while wiping away the self-editing efforts that come with lying. It's hardly any chemical truth serum. It's natural magic.

After I sprinkled the powder, I delivered the verse that engaged the spell. When I saw the bright, alert expression on Germani's face, I began the questioning.

"Did you kill the driver from your company on Ibis Drive?"

"I did."

"Why?"

"They switched routes on us at the last minute. Ben was going to take my truck because the packages were already loaded. The problem was, I was in the middle of using my truck to transport some junk from my house. It's on the market, you know."

"You killed him simply because he was going to use your truck?"

"Because if Ben saw the junk I had in it, I would have gotten into serious trouble."

"What, exactly, was the junk?" I asked.

"Remains of some of my victims."

"Murder victims?"

"Yeah, if you insist on calling them that."

"What would *you* call them?"

"Playthings."

"Man, that's sick," Matt said.

I shook my head at him for interrupting. The subject of my spell needed to be focused on me.

"Who were these victims?"

"Mostly random people I grabbed at night. Pizza delivery guys, runaways, parking-garage attendants. But I also found some during the day on my delivery routes. Like lawn guys who were alone in a backyard where no one could see them. You could say I grab easy opportunities that present themselves."

"We thought the missing people in Jellyfish Beach were mostly the victims of ghouls," I said. "You mean they were all *your* victims?"

"Even I am not *that* good. The freaking ghouls pick off vulnerable people at night, too. I guess you could say we're competitive predators."

"How did you kill Ben?" I demanded.

"I followed him in another truck. When he got to that address, I attacked him with my sword. It was the only weapon I had."

"All that was found at the scene was his leg. Where is the rest of him?"

"I don't know."

"What do you mean, you don't know?"

"He escaped."

"How did he escape? You took off his leg."

"I lost my balance and fell. He hopped away."

"He was hopping on one leg, and you couldn't catch him?"

"No. Guess I'm getting too old for this. He made it to a

neighbor's yard, then disappeared. I thought for sure I was about to be arrested, so I had to get out of there, but the police never came for me. Ben must have succumbed to his wounds somewhere."

I needed to investigate that. It freaked me out to think someone had died near my house and hadn't been found.

"After he escaped, you dumped remains you call 'junk' behind the house where you attacked him?" I asked.

"Yeah. Those old ladies are ghouls, so I figured I'd pin the murders on them."

"You know they're ghouls?"

"Of course. You saw what came through my fence just now. I have a ghoul problem here. They're like a rat infestation, but much deadlier. And every time I bury a body in the landfill, they sniff it out. They dig up and devour the body, then leave the remains in my yard. I know ghouls, all right. Even when they take on human form, I can recognize them."

"Why did you dump a bag of bones on my lawn? I'm not a ghoul."

"I knew you were investigating what happened to Ben. I wanted to put you on the defensive."

"You really thought it was believable that I would put human bones at the curb for trash collection?"

Germani shrugged, but there was an unsettling shift in his expression. The spell must be wearing off.

"One last question. Did you abduct Detective Shortle?"

"When she went behind your house, she presented a perfect opportunity. I didn't know she was a cop—I thought she was a realtor. My bad."

Yes, his bad.

"I'm going to call her now," I said. "You can apologize to her when she gets here."

A car roared down the road, braking hard, spraying a shower of dirt.

"That was fast," Germani said.

"I wish it was her," I said.

The car doors popped open, and three dorky guys jumped out.

The Knights Simplar.

"We meet again," said Lord Arseton.

He wore a fur suit, like a sports mascot, only he was missing the head. My guess was he was supposed to be a bear. His two goons were also in fur suits and had their heads on, probably because they weren't driving. The tall, stooped one was a red fox. The short, stout one appeared to be a dog.

"You guys didn't have to get all dressed up because of me," I said.

"We were at a furry convention," Lord Arseton said.

"Why?" Matt asked. "Not that there's anything wrong with that."

"I've already explained this," said Lord Arseton. "Religious worshippers and people who live in fantasy worlds all have strong belief systems, which attract supernatural entities and other misbegotten creatures. Our mission is to destroy them."

"Furries? Really? What do they have to do with the supernatural?"

"They attract various chimera—half-human, half-beasts."

"Have you bothered to look in a mirror?"

Arseton ignored me. "We have been following you, witch.

And we finally have proof now that you are a sorceress. We captured you on video, enchanting this poor man."

"He's a serial killer. Save your pity for someone else."

"He is?" the tall guy—I mean, fox—asked.

"Yeah." I glanced at Germani. The truth spell hadn't worn off fully. "How many victims do you have?"

"Um, I guess a couple dozen. But who's counting?"

"The police are, I can assure you."

"That is not our concern," Lord Arseton said. "Come with us, witch. We must interrogate you before we burn you."

"I don't think so," Matt said, brandishing Germani's sword.

Arseton laughed. "We're not at the Renaissance Festival, fool."

"This is the third time they've threatened us with a sword," the tall knight said.

He fumbled with his fox suit. Did it have pockets? Finally, he found an opening and pulled out his gun.

"Drop it," he said to Matt.

"You'll have to take it from me," Matt said, his sword arm quivering.

The two goons rushed him.

Matt swung his sword at the tall one and knocked off his fox head. The man's face was sweaty and embarrassed. Matt lunged and cut the fur suit on the man's abdomen before the two tackled him. The stout one in the dog costume hit him in the head with his pistol, and Matt went limp.

I ran to Matt and knelt to examine him. He had a serious contusion on his forehead, but was breathing regularly. His pulse was normal.

The tall one aimed his handgun at Matt and prepared to fire.

"No," Lord Arseton said. "We don't kill civilians."

He picked up the iron sword and flung it into Germani's yard.

"Let's grab her before she hexes us," he said, pointing at me.

All three knights rushed me. During our inane bantering, I'd been casting a protection spell, but it wasn't complete yet. I should have tried to run away, but I didn't want to leave Matt and break the immobility spell that had disabled Germani.

Lord Arseton grabbed me by the hair and pulled me to my feet while his goons seized my arms. They dragged me toward their car.

But they were distracted by the growling and hissing, the strange mewling and chittering.

I hadn't seen the ghouls sneak up on us—three of them had gotten through the fence and were almost upon us.

The iron sword was far out of reach. The three knights, plus Matt and I, were about to be devoured.

The tall goon fired his weapon at the nearest ghoul. It didn't even slow the monster down. Its glowing red eyes were fixated on the bloodstain on the man's fur suit. The ghoul opened its mouth, baring long, yellow, needle-like teeth. It reached for the man. He fired again. The ghoul seized him with its long fingers tipped with razor claws.

Wait—I recognized this ghoul. It was June.

And one of the other ghouls had a tuft of unnatural, platinum-blonde hair atop its bald head.

Alex. And the third one was May.

The Golden Ghouls were here to rescue us. Or maybe eat us all. I wasn't yet sure how it would play out.

The tall Knight Simplar screamed. Then, he was silent.

The three sisters crowded around him. He was gone faster than a donut in an office break room.

The stout one didn't even have time to fire his weapon before he was taken. He put up a good fight. But when it came to Prey vs. Predators, the Predators were now winning 2 - 0.

Lord Arseton didn't achieve the status of self-proclaimed lord by being stupid. He bolted, whimpering in panic, to the car. He drove away before the ghouls finished with his second knight.

And now, the only human left standing was me. Matt moaned on the ground, slowly regaining consciousness. Germani was still bound by my spell.

The ghouls turned their attention to me.

The iron sword was dozens of feet away.

"Hey, girls, it's me, Missy. Your neighbor. You remember me, right? I'm the one who's been working to exonerate May. You don't want to eat me. I'm just skin and bones, anyway."

"We know," said Alex-ghoul in a scratchy voice.

The three ghoul sisters raised their bony arms in a semblance of a wave.

They retreated through the hole in the fence and disappeared into the night.

"What happened?" Matt asked with a groan as he sat up on the ground.

"My ghoul neighbors ate two of the Knights Simplar but spared us. I suspected May had been hiding out here at the landfill, so I asked Alex and June to send her here to lure

Germani out of his house. Alex and June came along to monitor things. I'm glad they stuck around to save us from those three weirdoes."

"I'm glad they didn't eat us, too."

"Yeah. And I wasn't positive they wouldn't." I glanced at Germani. He was still immobile. "I wish the police would get here."

"Hey, won't you let me go, please?" Germani asked. "I'll pay you a hundred grand."

Yeah, right. Obviously, the truth-telling spell had completely worn off.

"You don't have that kind of money."

"But I will. As soon as my house sells."

"I believe property that's a crime scene might take a little longer to sell than you think."

CHAPTER 24
BURIED SECRETS

I needed to consult two different grimoires, but I finally pieced together instructions for making a certain amulet.

My vampire-repellant amulets had proven to be unreliable. (Thank you, Mrs. Steinhauer.) This one had better work, though it had a different target.

It was meant to repel werewolves.

"I don't want any Girl Scout cookies," Fred Furman said when he answered the door.

He looked surprised to see it was me.

"You're the woman who lives one block over, right?"

"Yes. Missy Mindle. We met last week when we spied on the Osmans eating barbecue ribs."

"Ah, yes. Now I remember. Are you here with good news, like those ghouls all getting arrested?" Rather than invite me in, he stepped onto his front porch and closed the door.

"The other Osmans have not been arrested," I said. "It turns out the murderer is a human. A delivery driver. He dumped the bag of remains in the Osmans' garden to shift blame to them. He knew they're ghouls."

"Then, who killed him in their yard?" Furman asked.

"The man who was killed was a different driver. He accidentally took the murderer's truck, which had the remains of his victims in it. So, the murderer attacked him in the Osmans' yard. He hoped to make it look like ghouls did it."

"You're gonna have a hard time convincing me the ghouls didn't do it."

"The victim was attacked with an iron blade. Iron is anathema to ghouls. They couldn't have used such a weapon."

"I'm sure the ghouls told you that. Don't be so fast to believe them."

"The guy who bought the iron sword also told me. He uses it against ghouls himself."

"I need to get me one of those. Well, even if they didn't kill that guy in their yard, I'm sure they ate him."

"No, they didn't," I said. "And he didn't die in their yard."

Furman tensed. "What do you mean?"

"The victim was badly wounded in the Osmans' yard, but he managed to escape into the property behind it."

"Wait, you're talking about *my* property? That's impossible. I have a fence."

"Mr. Furman, he could have simply gone around the fence through your next-door neighbor's yard."

"Well, I never saw him in my yard. He must have passed through quickly."

"No. I think he never left your property alive."

Furman's eyes squinted beneath his bushy white eyebrows.

237

"Are you accusing me of something? Who are you to come to my house and make unfounded accusations?"

"If you shifted to wolf and ate the man, you're putting the supernatural population of Jellyfish Beach at significant risk."

Furman waved his hand dismissively. "You're a nutcase. Get off my property."

"The man who tried to murder the victim has undoubtably told the police the same story—that his would-be victim escaped into your yard and then disappeared. The police will search your property."

"Get out of here or I'm calling the cops."

He turned away and slammed the door in my face. But before the door closed on me, I saw the fear in his face.

ONE OF THE wards I set in the Osmans' backyard alerted me it had detected noises coming from Furman's property. I hurried over to the Osmans' and went around the end of Furman's fence, just like the murdered delivery driver had done.

As I expected, Furman was digging a hole in his backyard.

He jumped when I turned on my flashlight and hit him with its beam.

"You get out of here!" he whispered loudly. "I'll call the cops."

I walked over to him and shined my light on the plastic leaf bag at the bottom of the hole.

"Yes, call them," I said. "So they can arrest you for killing and eating the delivery driver."

Furman crouched and held his shovel in a defensive position. I was wearing my werewolf-repellant amulet and had placed a protection bubble around my immediate body. However, I braced for Furman to hit me with his shovel or attack me in wolf form.

"I'm on the side of all supernatural creatures," I said. "It was wrong of you to have eaten that man, but I understand you might not always be in control while in wolf form. You weren't hunting humans; you were defending your territory from an intruder. I understand."

His body relaxed slightly, but he still seemed dangerous.

"The Friends of Cryptids Society told me they will not punish you. But if you kill another human, you will be forced to sell your home and leave the area."

Furman remained silent.

I held out a sheet of paper. "This is the address of the delivery driver who confessed to murdering several people. The police are only just beginning to search his home and property. Take these remains, and if the coast is clear, bury them on or near his property, as if he put them there himself. Otherwise, you'll be arrested for murder."

"Werewolves don't do well in jail," he whispered.

"No. The full moon will make sure of that."

"Would you believe me if I told you I found him dead on my lawn and buried him because it seemed like the right thing to do?"

"No, I would not believe you."

"Oh." He hung his head in shame. "He was dying anyway from the blood loss after losing his leg. I simply ended his suffering."

"Say what you will. He was alive when he entered your property."

I believed Furman that Nogging was already a goner when he entered the property. Severed arteries will do that to you. The only way to save him would have been the expert use of a tourniquet until paramedics arrived. Furman's werewolf instincts ruled that out.

Furman was guilty of eating the man, but Germani was clearly at fault. He was the murderer. Even in the morally gray world of cryptids, justice had been accomplished in my eyes.

"I haven't dined on a human since the Reagan Administration," Furman said. "I just couldn't help it. The scent of his blood drove me crazy. It's this Paleo diet I'm on. What a mistake!"

"I know you'll never let it happen again."

"No, I won't."

"Yeah, you won't," I said. "Or else you will be put down."

CHAPTER 25

YOU CAN ALWAYS FIND ME HERE

One morning, two months later, I opened the botanica, and my first visitor was not a paying customer. It was the attorney, Paul Leclerc. I was happy to see him.

"Good news or bad news for May?" I asked. He was one of those older, balding men who insisted on wearing a ponytail. You wouldn't think werewolves can go bald, but they do. Paul was an excellent lawyer, and the supernatural community depended on him.

"Yesterday was her last court hearing. The D.A. dropped the murder charge against her after Germani was arrested and confessed. He denies moving the delivery driver's body to his house, but the remains were found on his property. However, we still had to clear up the charges May faced for escaping from the jail."

"I know. I've been so worried about that."

"Well, we had a lot of luck in that the jail security cameras

241

didn't capture her supernatural form. That flaw in the technology has saved a bunch of my werewolf clients who were arrested and shifted while incarcerated."

"It doesn't change the fact she knocked the guards around like bowling pins and escaped."

"I think the warden is too embarrassed his guards were humiliated like that. Besides, May put on a good show, convincing the judge that she's just a sweet old lady who was worried about her sisters' safety."

"Are you saying she's off the hook for escaping?"

"All she got was probation and community service."

"She must have truly charmed the judge."

"And, well, my paralegal is a witch. She used an empathy spell on the judge."

"Oh, my."

"And before you question my integrity, we use that spell very sparingly when I'm in court. Never on a jury. Well, okay, only once or twice."

"So, the Golden Girls' lives are back to normal."

"Yes. You can expect an invitation to tea any day now."

"I can't wait." The sarcasm in my voice was too obvious.

I thanked Paul for giving me the news. Only minutes after he left, my next non-paying customers arrived.

Mrs. Lupis and Mr. Lopez surveyed the botanica.

"I see some improvements, but you haven't expanded yet into the space next door," said Mr. Lopez.

"Yeah," I said. "The former takeout-seafood restaurant.

We're having a hard time finding contractors who aren't super-stitious about botanicas. Plus, it still smells like rancid fryer oil over there, and it's overrun with roaches."

"Perhaps, you should simply knock it down and start fresh," Mrs. Lupis said.

"That's looking like a great idea."

"We have made inquiries into the Knights Simplar," said Mr. Lopez.

"Do they have anything to do with the Paladins? My neigh-bors suggested as much."

"They fancy themselves to be in the tradition of the Paladins of the Holy Sepulcher, who were founded during the Crusades to fight heretics and monsters. Until they all became vampires."

"And were staked by the Knights Templar," Mrs. Lupis added.

"Oh, my."

"The Knights Simplar are mostly misguided buffoons," Mr. Lopez continued. "The problem being that they are under the influence of a demon."

"Oh, my."

"Yes. We're uncertain why the demon is sending them after cryptids. We think the demon wants to create chaos by flushing the monsters out into the open."

"The Knights Simplar are cartoonish," said Mrs. Lupis. "But, under the influence of the demon, they can be extremely dangerous."

"They want to kill me."

"We are quite aware of that, Mr. Lopez said. "They need to be stopped. They lost two of their most fanatical members, but there are many more, and their leader is still in command."

"And how did they figure out so easily that I'm a witch?"

"The demon gives them magic. How much, we aren't sure."

"We will help you defend yourself if they attack again," said Mrs. Lupis.

"What am I supposed to do in the meantime?"

"Go about your life while staying vigilant. Until your next assignment presents itself."

"Presents itself?"

"Keep an eye out for new monsters to catalog," Mrs. Lupis said. "And you should lend your evidently quite impressive detective skills to any creatures or entities who need them."

"When we need you, we'll let you know," her partner added. "Chances are, it will be sooner than you think."

The two enigmas in the gray suits took their leave. I braced for an influx of rush-hour customers.

THE BELL over the door tinkled again. It wasn't a rush-hour customer.

Harry Roarke entered, his eyes widening as they roved the store.

"This place is weird," he said.

"No, it's not. Most botanicas look like this."

That wasn't exactly accurate. Most botanicas don't sell supplies for the types of witchcraft I do. And, of course, most don't have zombies wandering around. I glanced behind me to make sure Carl wasn't here.

"Do you like being a shopkeeper better than a nurse?" Harry asked.

"I'll always be a nurse at heart. And I'll always be available if you and Cynthia need me. Has Acceptance Home Care sent you a new nurse?"

He frowned. "Yeah. She's okay. Just a regular human and not a witch like you. Which is why I'm here." His frown turned into a huge smile. "The flea potion worked!"

"Good!" I'd been wondering about that. I had finished it and delivered it to the Roarkes in the middle of the murder investigation and hadn't had time to follow up with them.

"Knocked the fleas right off us, and they've never come back. Even after we went wilding in the nature preserve several nights in a row. I had some left over and gave it to Steve, the new werewolf from Wisconsin. It worked for him, too."

"I'm so happy to hear that."

"You know, word is getting around about the potion, and others have asked me about it. You could bottle it and make a fortune in the werewolf communities."

It was something to consider. If I could find a more affordable source of muskrat belly fur.

Harry thanked me again profusely and wasn't even out the door when Detective Shortle came in. She had the same reaction to the store that Harry had.

In my previous job, when no one knew whether I was home during the day or out seeing non-vampire patients, all people could do was call or text me. And there was a good chance I wouldn't answer right away. Now, everyone knew exactly where to find me.

"What can I do for you, Detective?" I asked with a genuine smile. "Are you in need of a charm or potion?"

She shook her head. "No, I'm just here to see where you work and to ask you a question. Remember, I swore that I would find out how you found me when I was a captive. Something tells me you practice magic—though I don't believe in it myself."

"I'm mostly into the healing arts, whether through medicine or spirituality."

"Yeah, whatever. Anyway, there have been some weird incidents lately that might have something to do with this world." She pointed to our aisles of merchandise.

"Like what?"

"Cow dung has been found at the doors of several houses of worship. They all serve different faiths, so the vandalism doesn't seem to be hate crimes."

"Well, that's not a ritual practiced by Santeria, voodoo, or any of the other religions our customers follow. This sounds to me like a case of teenagers playing tasteless pranks."

"Me, too. I just wanted to make sure it wasn't some kind of hoodoo or voodoo or whatever." She glanced at her phone. "I've got to go, but please let me know if you hear anything about this."

"I will."

After the bell tinkled as the door closed behind her, my mood turned dark. Yes, the cow dung sounded like it was from bored adolescents.

But black magic could also be behind it, especially since it involved houses of worship. And whenever I thought of black magic, I thought of my mother.

Was she involved with the poop vandalism? I hoped she wasn't, because if she were doing evil acts here in my territory, I would inevitably clash with her. There's no law that says white-magic witches must drive black-magic practitioners away, but it's necessary to protect the magic equilibrium. Even if it meant a deadly battle with my own mother.

Black magic pollutes and corrupts all magic.

Sometimes, however, I wondered if even good magic corrupts. You see, I wanted to grow as a witch, learning more spells and becoming more effective. That meant becoming more powerful. I told myself that the goal was to heal better, to keep my friends safe, to do good, and fight evil. I convinced myself that I had lofty motives, not selfish ones.

Yet, the fact was, magical power was intoxicating. The more you had, the more you wanted. It was too easy to crave power for power's sake.

And that was frightening. Because that was what had happened to my mother: she switched to black magic to gain more power, and it made her evil. People and other creatures suffered because of her magic.

I want magic to make me a better person, not a worse one, like my mother.

Using magic to affect the material and spirit worlds was risky. I must never forget that.

I RECEIVED one more non-paying customer.

"I hear your neighbor's legal troubles have been settled," said Matt, who came in wearing a big smile.

We gave each other quick pecks on the cheek.

"Yes, the ghouls can get back to their regular lives of pretending to be vegans. So, what brings you here? You just happened to be in the neighborhood?"

"Yes, and I realized I've never visited your store. It's so . . . unique."

"The name 'Mystical Mart and Botanica' sums it up nicely. There's something for everyone, from witches to voodoo practitioners."

"Can I get my fortune told here?"

"We don't have a psychic with a crystal ball, but you can set up an appointment with a spiritual advisor of whichever faith you desire."

"I think I'm good for now. Um, what are those statuettes over there?"

"They're Santeria orishas. Would you like a crash course in the Yoruba religion and the New-World religions that evolved from it?"

"Actually, I stopped by to ask you out on a date."

"Oh, really?" I made my best attempt at being coy.

But the mood was quickly dashed by the ringing of the bell above the front door and the eerie moaning.

"Omigod! Is that a zombie?" Matt asked before hyperventilating.

"That's Carl. And, yes, he's a zombie."

Carl wandered into the store. He must have forgotten something—not unusual with a zombie brain. Matt caught his attention. He probably sensed Matt was my friend because he shuffled toward him.

"Matt, meet Carl."

The sight of an elderly Haitian man in his black funeral suit and the half-rotting face was more than Matt could handle.

"Matt, he's harmless. You faced ghouls just the other night, and they're truly dangerous."

"Don't let him touch me," Matt said through clenched teeth.

He had backed up as far as he could go until his butt hit the front counter.

"Whaaargh?" Carl asked, reaching his putrid hand toward Matt's face.

"Missy, I'll call you later." Matt dodged Carl's hand and rocketed out of the botanica almost as fast as a vampire. The bells were still tinkling after he disappeared down the street.

Carl moaned.

"Yes, he does really like me," I said. "He's put up with years of me working the night shift for vampires and werewolves. And now, I've gotten him involved with ghouls, a demonic cult, and a zombie."

Carl made a cooing sound, not unlike a human baby.

"And he still wants to hang out with me. Go figure."

WHAT'S NEXT

Monsters of Jellyfish Beach Book 2:

A high-stakes vampire murder mystery.

I'm just your typical witch who owns an occult shop and catalogs monsters for a mysterious society. But now, I must play witchy private detective for a young woman trying to free herself from a vampire who mesmerized her after they met on a dating app.

Before I get the chance to work my magic, he is staked. My client is accused of the crime by the vampires' barbaric criminal justice system. And she's depending on me to prove her innocence and save her life.

The murdered vampire had dated many young humans

251

whom he later turned into vampires and dumped. All of them had motives to stake him. He was also a wealth manager for vampires—who need gigantic nest eggs to last them for eternity—and he defrauded several clients. Any of them could have staked him.

Meanwhile, storm clouds are brewing in Jellyfish Beach as my estranged mother returns to practicing black magic. And a sinister monster-slaying cult continues to stalk me.

On a happier note, the vampire creative writing group I supervise got a new member: a famous poet who was supposed to be buried 130 years ago. Too bad his genius hasn't rubbed off on the other members.

Dive into a wacky world of murder, magic, and mayhem with the "Monsters of Jellyfish Beach." Get them at Amazon or via wardparker.com

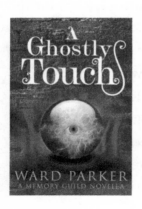

GET A FREE E-BOOK

Sign up for my newsletter and get *A Ghostly Touch*, a Memory Guild novella, for free, offered exclusively to my newsletter subscribers. Darla reads the memories of a young woman, murdered in the 1890s, whose ghost begins haunting Darla, looking for justice. As a subscriber, you'll be the first to know about my new releases and lots of free book promotions. The newsletter is delivered only a couple of times a month. No spam at all, and you can unsubscribe at any time. Get your free book for all e-readers or as a .pdf at wardparker.com

ACKNOWLEDGMENTS

I wish to thank my loyal readers, who give me a reason to write more every day. I'm especially grateful to Sharee Steinberg and Shelley Holloway for all your editing and proofreading brilliance. To my A Team (you know who you are), thanks for reading and reviewing my ARCs, as well as providing good suggestions. And to my wife, Martha, thank you for your moral support, Beta reading, and awesome graphic design!

About the Author

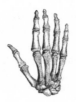

Ward is also the author of the Memory Guild midlife paranormal mystery thrillers, as well as the Freaky Florida series, set in the same world as Monsters of Jellyfish Beach, with Missy, Matt, Agnes, and many other familiar characters.

Ward lives in Florida with his wife, several cats, and a demon who wishes to remain anonymous.

Connect with him on social media: Twitter (@wardparker), Facebook (wardparkerauthor), BookBub, Goodreads, or check out his books at wardparker.com

PARANORMAL BOOKS BY WARD PARKER

Freaky Florida Humorous Paranormal Novels
Snowbirds of Prey
Invasive Species
Fate Is a Witch
Gnome Coming
Going Batty
Dirty Old Manatee
Gazillions of Reptilians
Hangry as Hell (novella)

Books 1-3 Box Set

The Memory Guild Midlife Paranormal Mystery Thrillers

A Magic Touch (also available in audio)

The Psychic Touch (also available in audio)

A Wicked Touch (also available in audio)

A Haunting Touch

The Wizard's Touch

A Witchy Touch

A Faerie's Touch

The Goddess's Touch

The Vampire's Touch

An Angel's Touch

A Ghostly Touch (novella)

Books 1-3 Box Set (also available in audio)

Monsters of Jellyfish Beach Paranormal Mystery Adventures

The Golden Ghouls

Fiends With Benefits

Get Ogre Yourself

Made in the USA
Las Vegas, NV
29 December 2023

83524135R00152